DANIEL – A LIFE

I0687015

Dorothy Davies

DANIEL – A LIFE

ISBN: 978-1-78695-181-6

Zadkiel Publishing
An Imprint of Fiction4All
www.fiction4all.com

This Edition
Published 2018

Part I - Life With Daniel

Chapter 1

This book is the story of a life.

In the first part it tells of the relationship between two people, one living, one 'dead' or, if you prefer, from both sides of the Great Divide. I am here, living in this material world and Daniel, my dear friend, is living in the spirit world. Together we relate how the book came to be written: the obstacles, the heartache, the sadness and the trauma of the telling of the sad tale and the lighter moments when Daniel took on his other persona, a clown. Daniel's life was unbelievably hard, unbelievably tragic and ended in the most horrific of circumstances. It was tough going from beginning to end, but as I said to Daniel after one emotional communication in Circle, I consider it an honour to have been selected to channel it for him.

For those who like to know how things happen: with all communications from spirit, I am aware someone wishes to 'write' when my hands start tingling and there is an overwhelming urge to clear the screen and simply type the date. Then the words come with such force that they have to be typed. Most people actually physically write with pen on paper but my writing is so bad, after so many years of typing, that it is illegible even to me. Spirit communicators know this and are happy to use the modern technology of the computer to get their message across.

This is how this book has been written. A pattern developed: I would deal with correspondence, maybe work on some other projects and then the tingling would begin and the book would continue its progress. Sometimes we would write a single line, other times a paragraph. Only toward the end of the book, as later communications show, did we ever reach the giddy heights of a page or more at a time. At the very end we were writing several pages at a time, but always it was difficult, always it was traumatic and always it was emotional.

It has been like reading a book rather than writing it, for I never knew what was coming next. In the early days, Daniel would often stop at a really critical point because he was unable to go on. Then the whole of the next section would be literally thrown at me, like a bucket of cold water, in a split second at some point when I was least prepared for it – making a cup of tea, about to turn over to go to sleep – and I would then be aware of the next painful instalment and be emotionally ready for the words when they came. It was as if Daniel needed to prepare me as much as himself for the next dreadful instalment of a nightmare of a life. When I received these blasts, I understood only too well why he had stopped and why he felt it necessary to prime me before carrying on. I was always grateful for the advance warning, for the time for mental preparation before once again channelling horrors of our modern world.

The book constantly surprised me, often moved me deeply and always interested me. That one person could suffer so much in one relatively short life is almost unbelievable. I 'wrote' it through a series of debilitating migraines, often in weariness after a day at work, always with New Age music to distract the thoughts as far as possible from the horrors which were being spelled out. Such is the closeness between Daniel and myself that migraines and tiredness made no difference to the flow of the book. If he was able to go on, we went on. Sometimes there were tears, from Daniel or from me or, at times, from both of us. There was one memorable night when I was so deeply involved in the book that, when I became aware of his tears, I reached for my handkerchief and handed it to him … If nothing else, it made him laugh.

From Day 1 the book has been called 'Daniel – a Life' and indeed it is hard now to remember a life without Daniel. A life when I did not, stage by painful stage, transcribe a book which at times was almost too much for both of us. When a medium did not turn to me on the platform where I chaired and asked: 'why do I see a harlequin clown around you?' Or my friend saying during my messages 'you know who's here and he's making me laugh.' A life when I did not at times feel fingers in my hair or hear an irreverent whisper in my ear. A time when I was not aware of a loving vibration around me. A time when I was not walking into a shop to buy a silly gift for my friend, the beautiful lady Daniel refers to, and finding myself wrapping the gift and adding the tag: *to the beautiful lady, with love from Daniel.* A time when, if something went missing, I had a pretty good idea who had taken it … It is very much as though he has always been there – the security is in knowing he always will be.

Life with Daniel is often fun - and that is something some mediums misunderstand. When I told one medium that Daniel often throws my soft toys around or hides things, she said: 'tell him to stop! You wouldn't allow a child to act that way, would you?" which completely missed the point that it was done to make me laugh and thus lift my spirits. I now know to be very careful to whom I mention such things …

I have had items mysteriously disappear and then re-appear in unlikely places, I have had the aerial on the radio suddenly fall down to startle me, heard creaks and clicks and have had such outrageous things whispered in my ear at times that it has been hard to keep a straight face. Once, when we had a large circle, he went round the entire group and made wicked comments about every sitter, which meant I could not pass on what was I receiving ...

But to start at the beginning ...

I came into Spiritualism in October 1995, after Spirit gently nudged, pushed and coerced me into attending a Spiritualist church for the very first time. It was a shock to the system for it was just like coming home and I knew then I had found the movement I needed to fulfil my spiritual yearnings.

I subsequently moved from the Development Circle at that church to a Home Development Circle, where the atmosphere and the sitters were quite different. The medium whose home we used and whose Circle it was, has a psychic drawing of one of his guides. One night he brought the picture down to show us and one of the sitters said she could see faces in the drawing. She went home to draw what she had seen.

Each time she drew someone, that guide would come through at Circle, but only after we had the drawing in our hands. One time she came with a drawing which she said looked like Mozart to her, she had music and the year 1700 associated with it. That drawing turned out to be Daniel.

From that time I have received a steady stream of communications, both written and verbal, some recorded in circle, some whispered in my ear which were so irreverent I could not tell anyone about them. I also received mentions of Daniel from other communicators, which I have included so that the reader will know that he was around all the time; if not communicating himself, he was through others.

His first communication was in early 1997. He came as a joker, making us laugh, making comments about each one of us.

(Unfortunately, the tape of that first communication is not available. If you listen to the recording that does exist, you can hear the distinct *clunk* of a tape being stopped dead for no reason other than the fact Spirit did not want that particular communication recorded. This is a phenomena we have experienced many times in circle, it is a shame that the first communication is not available, but it lives on in my heart and mind in any event.)

***

A thought occurred (or an idea implanted) during the writing of the book, is that Daniel deliberately came as a clown to find out who would accept him. It was a test. He had been rejected by many circles and almost rejected by ours because he did not come as a serious guide, imparting philosophy which we could accept. He came as himself, or at least one side of him, looking for people who would accept him as Daniel, a spirit with a serious problem that needed love, consideration and understanding to resolve. Circles, it would seem, are 'conditioned' into expecting serious guides and perhaps tend to resent those who aren't as serious as the sitters think they should be. But this would exclude the delightful Micky, the guide and companion of Leslie Flint, for one! There are many others, including spirit children who come to give laughter and upliftment to the sitters.

There were two sides to Daniel, as there are to all of us, but with him it was very pronounced. He was either a clown or a depressive discarnate spirit still coming to terms with the tragedies, the horrors, the nightmares of his last incarnation. Something in me reached out to this troubled soul; we made contact and we have stayed in contact ever since.

When Daniel was sure of us, he came through one night on the very sad vibration I was to learn only too well over the years that followed. The other side of

Daniel was revealed, the side which cried out for love and cried out for me to hold him close, something I was unable to do. A transcript of this communication follows.

A comment on the communication: I should explain the picture. Our medium and Circle leader has a psychic drawing of one of his guides. One of the Circle sitters regularly 'saw' faces in this picture and would draw them. Later that guide would come through at circle. One was of Daniel, before he came. Once a guide was known, the picture would be framed and hung on the wall. The medium's wife appears to have banged the nail for Daniel's picture rather hard ...

2nd May 1997

It is I, Daniel, that speaks to you. The instrument's voice that I entrust to speak through is croaky due to a throat problem. So the earthly medium is needing healing. Your healing energies and mine. I, Daniel, along with all the others who bring this gift of healing to the sick of your world will channel the healing to where it is needed and to the earthly medium whose voice box I use, in order for communication between the two worlds to take place.

For usually I, Daniel, bring you laughter and upliftment but this night will you please be there for Daniel. For I need love, laughter and understanding. I have told you that out of many reincarnations upon earth within your material world of living that there was one reincarnation that has truly hurt me, has been impossible for I, Daniel, to come to terms with. I understand your uncertainty towards me for when I come and speak to you all, I do so to lift your vibrations. Some of you do not even like me. That is the impression I get. I am sorry for when my picture was put up on the wall, I thought I was going through into the adjacent room, as it was put up with so much force and anger. But the one who hung it is very sensitive, is very caring, is loving but does not like Daniel. I will not hurt, it is not in my nature to hurt. I have been hurt and could not possibly hurt others.

Daniel has a very soft nature, is very loving and cares. Yet the one who sits next to the instrument I entrust to speak through is also unsure of me and does not like me. In time you will all grow to like me.

I come to speak to you this evening for I need your loving vibrations, your love and understanding. I need to hear your laughter and your voices for it is good for me to be close to you, for this evening it is your turn to allow your healing rays and energies to flow through the instrument I speak through. I, Daniel, trust wholly in the instrument. Please give your love, your understanding, to Daniel, for I had a lot of reincarnations, some going back centuries, thousands of years. Indeed, one before the one a lot of people on your plane call the Master Jesus.

The reincarnation that I have been unable to come to terms with is the one where I was a prisoner in a German concentration camp in the last World War. A terrible experience; many horrific happenings took place. Men, women and young children were tortured and abused and then sent to the gas chambers to die. You have all read accounts of the war through books and you must be familiar with the name of Odette Churchill, who spent a long time as a prisoner in German concentration camps through World War Two. This brave lady wrote diaries of the accounts of the sadistic tortures. They pulled her fingernails out one by one, her toenails one by one. She was abused mentally and sexually. Books do not convey to you the whole truth. For young women, beautiful and young, were abused by the German officers, and by the high-ranking British officers who were given favours by their counterparts and so took part in the tortures in order to save themselves, cowards, like so many in your modern day of living. Daniel was there. I saw and witnessed every single act. It was degrading, cruel, mentally unbearable. Please forgive me for being blunt and to the point: young women of child-bearing age were continually used for sex by the high-ranking German officers and soldiers. These poor young women, beautiful women, most of them of Jewish nationality, were abused. There is another word for it. I am crying for I am ashamed to have had to witness such atrocities but was helpless to help. Once these young women were pregnant they were moved to separate quarters and when close to termination, were taken by train to the gas chambers where they would be killed.

It is not easy to convey to you what happened, for whilst these acts were going on, we would be stripped naked and lined up and had to watch degrading sex acts taking place. Women officers of the German army, which we took to be prostitutes, would come and abuse our bodies. It was so degrading. We had to witness women being forced to have sex during their monthly problems; there was no escape for if they refused, they were savagely beaten. It turned one's mind and on top of all this there was the sadistic torture. Young children didn't escape. Torture would include hot needles in the centre of one's eyes.

I have not been able to come to terms with this last reincarnation upon earth. Yes, I was frightened. The main prisoner of war camp that I was held in was not far from a place you know as Dortmund. There were many camps. I escaped on one occasion but through my love for others was recaptured and again tortured and abused. I did not survive the war, for the second time that I escaped I was shot three times.

Many ghastly happenings took place, we all suffered. For a time I was moved from camp to camp. I had the privilege of meeting brave men and women who suffered for their country. Odette Churchill, a brave lady whom I was honoured to come into contact with, all that she wrote was true but even some atrocities were kept from you, the secretness of nations and those who govern will not take the blame.

In later communications I will tell you more. It still upsets me. This account has brought you tears, unhappiness that people, human beings, can go through much suffering and pain. Perhaps you have learned to like Daniel a little more. You have helped me for you have listened, for I have been trying through circles of light such as yours since my passing to unburden my problems, but those of higher understanding have not listened and have sent me on my way, empty.

You have listened to Daniel. You have accepted me. I thank you, for I have now been able to start to release my frustrations, anger, guilt and hatred for not only what happened to me but thousands and thousands of other men women and children.

You are very understanding, sensitive, loving people; the one who was very rough with my picture now likes me a little, understands now, feels for me.

Thank you for your time to listen to Daniel. I constantly relive those seconds, minutes, hours, days, months and years in the concentration camps, cannot really clear away the atrocities which took place. It is as if they are still happening. You have helped me a lot but there is still a lot to be unburdened.

The instrument I entrust to speak through to you will be cross for he has a throat problem this evening. I have made him work, I will return to speak to you very soon. I am pleased to have been with friends. Please take my love, friendship and compassion. Daniel leaves you all fully protected, none more than the entrusted instrument I speak through.

Daniel takes his leave.

Chapter 2

A short time later Daniel visited us again.

Good evening, it is I, Daniel.

Thank you for listening to me. It was much appreciated. I am with tears and with happiness this evening, it is a very difficult vibration for me to come in on but I understand now why the one who put my picture up with such gusto, such anger that I felt I was going from one room into another, my head was spinning but I can understand because this is how she has been feeling and it is... it is wrong. For you can only take so much and there has to be a parting of the waves, a parting of ways, a parting of the waves of the ocean. There had to be in my case, all I suffered in those concentration camps, there was only so much one could take and it is the same sort of feeling that the one who nearly threw Daniel's picture to kingdom come and back, it is how she feels. She has been treated in a very, very bad way by many. It does not do one any good to be continually mistreated, being spoken about, nasty words, wrongful actions, for this one is, as I have said, caring, loving, sensitive, would do anything for anyone.

It is time to move on, to put all the worry, all the unnecessary problems, hurt, to one side and move on, for by throwing my picture - not exactly throwing but letting your frustration, your anger, out into the open you had eventually allowed Daniel to come close to you, to help you overcome certain problems for I can give you that strength, that push, to get you over certain problems. But remember that the words you might utter to others are not your words, they're Daniel's because I am a little bit forward in what I say. You have been a little more outright with what you have said to certain ones

14

recently, is that not right? Answer Daniel, please. I am your friend. You know who I am talking to. She is deep in thought.

(the tape ends here)

***

The first deeply emotional communication was published in the October-November 1997 edition of the church newsletter which I was then editing, with this addition:

On the 18th May 1997 a medium, Hazel Butterworth, came to serve the church for the weekend. Over lunch we were discussing circles and guides. I began to tell her about Daniel and his last communication.

She suddenly stopped eating and looked at me in shock. Two days earlier she had woken with the Jewish song from 'Fiddler On The Roof' running through her mind, to find a man standing in her room, dressed, as she described it, in striped pyjamas. He was thin, bald, as if had endured chemotherapy, and had intense piercing eyes. He said 'hello' in a way that indicated she should have known who he was. She asked two people but they had no idea who he was.

The medium had been sending out thoughts to a Daniel, an old friend of hers, and it would seem she had attracted the Daniel we knew at Circle. Or Daniel appeared to her as proof for us. Whichever way round it was, she had not connected the 'striped pyjamas' with a concentration camp outfit, nor his emaciation and baldness as a result of his internment, which is understandable, as that is not the first thing you would think of. When I mentioned the concentration camp, it all came together: the Jewish song and his appearance.

And I, in turn, was experiencing the odd 'coldness' which told me I was being directed. We both had to share that revelation, it was proof for both of us and for those we will continue to tell about this.

Daniel gave his permission for the account to be used in the church newsletter in an equally emotional communication on the 18th July 1997, for I would not include it until he said I could. He wished people to read it and think of the cruelty which still goes on in our modern world and to do what we can to stop it.

I am aware that some people at the church doubted this communication, which hurt both of us very much, especially Daniel, who had to overcome his own emotional state in order to bring the communication to us. But truth will always be doubted.

***

It is only now, looking back through the many communications I have received, have I appreciated how many times Daniel has been mentioned by other guides – as if reassuring me of his constant presence and friendship, not that I ever doubted it for a moment. Here are a few examples from a Cardinal who worked with me at that time:

Cardinal Thomas Lindenwood; March 30th, 1998 -

In a discussion about guides: 'Daniel, your clown, comes when you need upliftment and oh yes, sister, he will work with you when the time is right. You are drawing closer all the time.'

Cardinal Thomas Lindenwood, 6th May 1998 -

In an encouraging communication when I was struggling with the end of my Aromatherapy course: 'Your cousin is watching over you, wanting to encourage you, guide you through the pitfalls of the last few weeks. Listen to him. He will be there with you as will Daniel and all of us, we are always around you.'

Cardinal Thomas Lindenwood, 8th May 1998 -
'Daniel sends his love, too.'

Cardinal Thomas Lindenwood, 26th May 1998 -
Another encouragement communication, designed to lift my spirits: 'Daniel is close, he says to thank you for the huge outpouring of love at the weekend, which lifted him so much and which healed much of his sadness.'

And Daniel himself, on the 17th July 1998
Well, well, well, it's Daniel, I've been trying to get through this evening through my sister here but she's just not coming through so I've had to come through him again. It's a bit noisy here tonight, isn't it?

Dorothy – Hello, Daniel.

Daniel - You were supposed to speak, I told you this morning.

Dorothy - Yes, I know.

Daniel - Yes, I've been with you all morning.

Dorothy - I know.

Daniel - You always say, 'I know.' Got an old girl here tonight, oh dear, got trouble with her false teeth as if she is losing her teeth. Oh dear, is that birds chirping I can hear?

Dorothy - Yes.

Daniel - Oh dear, rowdy, isn't it?

Circle sitter – Mmm.

Daniel - Who said Mmm?

Circle sitter – I did.

Daniel – Who's I?

Circle sitter – Me.

Daniel – Oh, yes. You see, I come through on a happier vibration tonight but it's her who should have

17

been doing it, not me. Because that was the intention right from the start. But I've come through with a bit, hm, not such a feminine side tonight, I've come through as Johnny, as a clown, yes, you were the one who nearly threw my picture through the wall.

Circle sitter - That's right.

Daniel –You never did like me, did you, but you stomach me now. The one beside you was just as bad, from what I remember. Can I hear a voice as well, will you speak to Daniel?

Another Circle sitter - I wasn't as bad as that, Daniel, I was the one who helped you come through.

Daniel – You might have helped but you didn't help this evening, it was a bit rough on the back seat of the car, you know, I should have come by myself on my own steam, but I thought, there is she is, I'll jump in, but you don't half drive fast, don't you? *(She laughs)*

Dorothy - You usually complain about my driving, don't you?

Daniel – I keep away. I like fast driving but I prefer to be with the one this evening and not you, sister.

Dorothy - You did say I was getting better.

Daniel - I don't like it when you cut the corners, you understand? We're going straight in a line and then - whoops - we're on the other side of the road!

Dorothy – It's legal if there's nothing there.

Daniel – Rubbish! It's dangerous; I jump out and go into the trees.

Dorothy - It's good to speak with you.

Daniel – Well, you're not getting away with it, I'm going to switch to you in a moment. That will be clever, won't it?

Dorothy – It will!

Daniel - I've just come from another lady like you, she's got to be pushed at times. Well I've been talking to you, sister.

Dorothy -Yes.

Daniel - And you've been writing.

Dorothy – Yes.

Daniel - Did you bring what I told you to write?

Dorothy - No.

Daniel - Oh dear. Good stuff, isn't I?

Dorothy -Yes.

Daniel – That's not me.

Dorothy -Then who is it?

Daniel -That's for you to find out. You can say it's through Daniel.

Dorothy - More work.

Daniel - It's all work. It's from somebody I was very close to. You know where I got this closeness to spirit because I wasn't always like this, you know. You see, we come through, we speak, I come through on a different vibration to lift you except when I tell you about my time in the concentration camp which was my last incarnation upon earth then I get very sad, sister. I'm not going to get sad tonight, because I come in on this vibration to lift you all. You've all been having trouble with your cars, haven't you? You could line them all up! Oh dear, oh dear. I think I'll come under my own steam next time. Mm. Come on then, I'm switching! Don't huff and puff, girl, just get on with it: it's there!

Dorothy – *(inaudible)*

Daniel – We spoke about it this morning.

(interruption)

Daniel - You can be quiet as well while we're talking!

Circle sitter – Could I ask a question?

Daniel – Don't think I'm going to answer it! Go on then.

Circle sitter – Before you transfer?

Daniel – Pardon?

Circle sitter – Before you transfer.

Daniel – I'll transfer to you if she doesn't speak up!

Circle sitter – Oh no, don't, don't do that. I'm not capable.

Daniel - Oh you've been told before what you can do.

Circle sitter – Were you, were you Mozart in a past life? One of your lives?

Daniel - Was I Mozart?

Circle sitter – Yes.

Daniel - Who the —— hell was Mozart? Sorry, my language.

Circle sitter - He was a composer.

Daniel - That's all right, I was testing you. No, I was not Mozart. Do I look like Mozart?

Circle sitter – In the drawing you do.

Daniel - You drew me? When did you draw me?

Circle sitter – When you first came into circle. And I got the year 1700 and I got music and harps with you and I thought you could have been Mozart in a past time.

Daniel - I am fond of poetry but what I am given is not through me if you understand. The sister knows, because it can be quite evidential writing that I give to her. It can also at times be in the form of poetry but we are still knocking on her door. Is there anybody in?

Dorothy - I am here and waiting.

Daniel – I am switching …

Dorothy - Why isn't it working then?

Daniel – Because you all keep speaking -

Daniel (through Dorothy) – The many conversations we have had, talking about this, going in and out but she is busy, busy, busy all the time and I have to try and get through and it isn't right and I am very tired and so I gave her a challenge tonight and it makes a change ... but we are going to write, Sister is going to write and I am going to write with her. … it will be interesting it will be good and you are all going to read it … I like the sound of the voices, I like to be here, I like to make you all happy ... *(unfortunately the tape has much background noise and much cannot be transcribed but it is obvious Daniel is speaking through Dorothy at that time. He then switches back to his first channel.)*

Daniel (through the channel) You are still quiet, have we shaken you?

Circle sitter - Yes you have.

(Dorothy is laughing)

Daniel - Well, Sister is laughing, she has not laughed for a long time like this, for every day I am with her, I try to make her laugh but it is difficult. You all need laughter, is that not so? Mm. The ride was uplifting *(more laughter)* you are all quiet, for one has not uttered one word. You may be content, so may others, but one was not uttered a word. He is still not uttering a word.

Circle sitter - One is listening.

Daniel - One is listening, one is bored, one has gone to sleep!

Circle sitter - One is listening.

Daniel - One is listening - But he won't help you either. My joke, I am sorry. *(much laughter)* It is good for there is laughter from another sister, see, she has needed laughter as well. The brother needs laughter. The one who threw my picture through the wall with such intensity is laughing.

(Circle sitters dissolve into laughter.)

Daniel - I still look beautiful, don't I, in that picture? There are many of those pictures, you know, but the one who draws has doubted herself, is this not so?

Circle sitter - Yes at times, but I've lost them.

Daniel - She must draw some more.

Circle sitter - You're not going to tell me where I've lost them.

Daniel - That would be too easy. You have not lost them, you are in such a muddle -

Circle sitter - Oh dear …

Daniel – I should not really say this -

Circle sitter - But you probably will

Daniel - But you've got a job to find your own clothes at times.

Circle sitter - Yes I know.

Daniel - So how can you find the pictures?

Circle sitter - They're not at home, I'm sure.

Daniel - They are. Very close to you. Just look.

Circle sitter - Thank you. I don't know where they are, I've looked and looked.

Daniel - Look again, they will fall out, your pictures, that is. *(Laughter)* oh dear, they are all asleep. I quite like that Mohican guy. (*the first communicator of the evening*) My sister, she needs the laughter, she needs this vibration of laughter. ...

Dorothy – You are often in my head, Daniel, it is good, isn't it, that we can speak to each other.

Daniel - Well, you see, if I am in your head, I cannot get out so I have to find another way of communication; but from the first time that I came to speak to you not many are left, did you frighten them all away?

Dorothy - They have all left.

Daniel - For a reason, for a reason ... For at times you have to be near the greater warmth and a greater understanding of people if you want to develop, do you understand and you cannot – I always said I would not bring in philosophy, what are you doing to me?

Dorothy - You always said that, but I will make a philosopher of you.

Daniel - It is the one who threw my picture through the wall who did that. What a lovely laugh! Did you hear that laugh?

Dorothy - I did.

Daniel – The laughter of a small child. That Mohican's coming back. Yes. Do you not all feel uplifted?

Circle sitters - Yes

Daniel - One is not speaking again. It's a lady this time.

Circle sitter – I'm relaxed.

Daniel –You're relaxed. That is good to hear. The gentleman's still quiet. He's pondering.

Circle sitter -Yes

Daniel - He's pondering. *(much laughter from circle members)* He doesn't sit still, you know.

Circle sitter - He tries.

Daniel - Twice?

Circle sitter - He tries.

Daniel - I am not deaf but I am a long way away from you. You disappeared when I was talking this morning, Sister. Where did you go?

Dorothy - Busy working, wasn't I?

Daniel - I should have been with you. Perhaps I couldn't go where you went.

Dorothy - You are often around me.

Daniel - I am there constantly, you know that

Dorothy – Yes. You also know I love you and I will work with you.

Daniel - The warmth is there for me. For I can go back to a time when like Daniel you needed that upliftment as you needed that closeness.

Dorothy - We will write the book.

Daniel - We will write the book and you will know the one who gives Daniel the words. Probably wrong for Daniel to say it was his work. Do you understand? You have been told this by me.

Dorothy - I know who works with me

Daniel - And you will find that the one who works with me is the one that Daniel was close to in that prison camp

Dorothy – Right.

Daniel - And all truths will be revealed. I am going home. I am tired.

23

Dorothy - Yes, it has been lovely.

Daniel - It has been hard work because I have been in three places this day and I have to return to where I came from this morning and I am late and I shall be told off. For she is with you shortly and she will talk about Daniel when she visits as she did before. It will be good for she is a beautiful lady. Are you going to say goodbye, Sister?

Dorothy - No, I am not going to say goodbye, because you are always with me.

Daniel - Are you going to let Daniel go or does Daniel have to say goodnight through the other channel? I will just say goodnight to you all. And stop walking about, the gentleman, get it sorted, all will be well. And you did well last night because I was with you.

Circle sitter - Thank you.

Daniel - That is all right. I walk with you as well to give you that upliftment as well because I come to you in your sad times and you do get those sad times but they will be far and few between. Just let the old go; the new is for you - the new is for Daniel. Cheerio then.

And a communication the following week...

Well, well, well, it's Daniel. I am sorry, Sister, that I came with such a negative vibration earlier on but you realise why; because of my time in the prisoner of war camp and you understand that the philosophy, the words that I am giving to you are not from Daniel, it is from a very, very dear lady who I had the pleasure of meeting. She was tortured, she was sexually abused, she had her toenails and fingernails taken out. She was badly tortured and this is why when I come in on that vibration you may think I come in very negatively, but you understand.

Dorothy – Yes I do.

Daniel - That is good: you all understand Daniel now. Even the one - I must keep stressing this - who threw my picture through the wall with great ferocity even speaks to Daniel now and that is good. But it is the lady who is giving Daniel the words, for Daniel does not give philosophy, Daniel's task is to uplift you and if I go on I must apologise but the lady comes in close to give you, my sister, the words. You all know her, do you not?

(general comment of Yes)

Daniel - Will tell you who she is, Odette Churchill and you may find that in time it will only come in small writings, do you understand?

Dorothy – Yes.

Daniel - But you may have to ask for permission because of the association of Odette Churchill and your past governments, do you understand? But you are very clever and that is why Daniel has come to you for these writings you understand?

Dorothy - I understand.

Daniel - Good evening (*here Daniel named one of the sitters directly*).

Circle sitter -Good evening, Daniel.

Daniel -There is another one who disliked me, perhaps still cannot take to Daniel, but you are honest, are you not?

Circle sitter - I hope so.

Daniel -You do not hope so, you are, for you do so much for people. I have got people playing with me tonight, I've got two three, dear oh dear, I've got a telling off from the beautiful lady.

Dorothy - It is open war.

Daniel - It is open war and it has been going on all week and insults have been going on between us and I am sure that shortly she will talk about Daniel to you again. We have been throwing quite a few nuts symbolically, but I have people on your side and from the realms playing games this evening because I have father, a father figure with me who says I do not like the beard, the mother says it's beautiful.

(Male sitter with new beard laughs)

Daniel - It is good to hear you laugh and I see what looks like a funny boat almost hitting what looks like to be a pier this day, it must have come in far too fast, can you relate to this, please?

Another sitter replies - I can.

Daniel - You can. I expect the people on board were quite frightened.

Circle sitter - They waved when it went past ...

Daniel - The instrument I speak through has had a turbulent day, oh dear oh dear, has he had to take some stick, not from the gentlemen but it was all ladies, oh dear! I have been quite busy this week for the one who cleanses gets all the rubbish all the negativity out of houses which are possessed or are haunted, she has surprised me but I have enjoyed it. I think she has got a room that needs sorting but Daniel needs help - it is - what do you call a small room within your houses on earth, a larder?

Dorothy - Box room.

Daniel - Oh yes it was not a larder, I could see no food. It is a box room. Daniel knows that there is the young girl of the age of six when she passed over from your earth to where Daniel resides now and it is as if she cannot let go. Would you concentrate your thoughts, your given gifts and your love for this young woman for she is constantly to and fro, like you on your material life as well, to and fro, to and fro for there is no time for anything it would seem, your life is busy.

(Comment made) Very.

Daniel - But she cannot let go. Who has just had their hair done then? *(silence)* Nobody will speak to Daniel. Who washed their hair today?

Circle sitter - It's not me, Daniel, that's for sure.

(Comments from sitters inaudible.)

26

Daniel - The gentleman and the lady perhaps? *(Names lady sitter again)* you should wash yours! My joke.

Circle Sitter - Yes, it's about time. I didn't have time tonight.

Daniel - You still drive fast. I did say I would not travel with you again but it wasn't so bad as last week.

(Another lady sitter wished a question answered.)

Daniel - You may ask me a question but I am not one who speaks on philosophy so I do not know what you are going to ask me and Daniel does not know if he can answer, do you understand?

Circle Sitter - Earlier on in the meditation I was shown a big boulder … *(inaudible but something to do with landslides)*

Daniel - I have been impressed when with you, perhaps you have not felt my closeness to you for you too when you first heard Daniel, you were probably unsure of Daniel's role, do you understand?

Circle Sitter – Yes.

Daniel - But I have to go back and I have to ask someone who is much more advanced than Daniel the answer to your question but I am asking for there is a wise Chinese philosopher-teacher who is coming close to Daniel and he is saying that when you see such as what you have described you are not very often wrong, do you accept this?

Circle Sitter – Yes.

Daniel - It is he who is telling me it is a minor earthquake but with not such a great loss of life as before but they are working through you in order for you to be able to put into words for people of that area of what you have seen

Circle Sitter -Thank you.

Daniel - And the impact will not be so great: it is what the Chinese philosopher is telling me. He gives the name of Chan Lee the Second.

Circle Sitter -Thank you, Daniel.

Daniel - It is time for Daniel to go home to look after the one I have caused turmoil to this day, I will get scolded. Daniel needs a drink because the instrument Daniel speaks through has a throat problem and could you pass a drink - all is well, thank you. *(Speaking to Dorothy)* You too need this laughter, this upliftment, do not be sad, none of you be sad, be happy. *(tape clicks off)*

Chapter 3

In 1998 I began channelling Daniel's life story. In between the actual writing of the book, Daniel would give me communications, some very personal. At times there appears to be long gaps between the written communications I have included here: I would not want you to think he was not there. This is the reason mention of him by other guides has been included.

Cardinal Thomas Lindenwood, 20th July 1998 -
A personal communication to calm my troubled mind, which actually started 'It is I, Thomas ...' which showed Daniel's influence and the mention of Daniel was in the second sentence: 'Our dear brother Daniel succeeded in making you laugh last week and was right when he said you had not laughed much lately. ... The beginning of the book for our brother Daniel is good, he is pleased with progress and you will write more and more as time goes on, when there is enough peace and time to do it.'

Cardinal Thomas Lindenwood, 22nd July 1998 -
Another personal communication – my guides give them to me for consolation and for peace of mind, for I am often troubled by many worries and thoughts which will not go away. 'You need to write some more book for our brother Daniel, with regret I must let you go. I could stay with you, writing words all night, but there will be other times, other opportunities, to give you the communications you need for our book. Yes, Daniel, I too will have a book!'

29th July 1998 - Cardinal Thomas Lindenwood,

'This strictly personal communication is now ending, as Daniel wishes to come close and get on with his book.'

We were working on the book fairly regularly, sometimes as little as a few lines or a paragraph at a time, sometimes quite a lot, so we were communicating virtually all the time. Because of this, Daniel did not always feel the need to come and give me specially written communications.

But when he did, they were usually pertinent and often deeply personal. Because of this, not every communication has been included and those that have may well have had certain lines removed for the sake of privacy and confidentiality.

This seems an appropriate moment to say that one medium rubbished the comment that my guide, Cardinal Thomas Lindenwood, said he liked the colours around my computer screen (purple). She said spirit guides were not interested in our daily lives, only in transmitting philosophy.

My answer now to that medium is that if you make a friend of your guides, not treat them as a book of philosophy which you open when needed, they do become interested in your daily lives, share with you the trials and tribulations of living on this earth plane, are there with sometimes personal comments about my fingernails, about work I have to do, like watering my courtyard full of potted plants, and so on. Daniel is not a guide: he is a friend, a dear and much loved friend, so he would certainly be interested in all that I do. And I in turn share my life with him.

Daniel often visited me at work, because I spend a considerable amount of time in front of the computer there. My office walls were hung with pictures, among which were several clowns, as well as the psychic portraits of Daniel himself. It is there Daniel often played some of his tricks …

Among other things, I am an Aromatherapist. My (non-believing) partner had a massage one afternoon and went off to comb his hair and sort himself out afterwards. When he came back, I commented that his trainers were undone and asked if he had in fact not tied them.

"I did," he said, "it's that damn clown of yours!"

The following communication from Daniel was given in July 1998. It actually took until October 2000 for Odette to finally come to me herself, although she 'visited' me during a reading in 1999. The medium said she had a lady wearing a green and gold dress coming close to me, who would help me with the next book. I had to complete a book before the way could be cleared to really work with Daniel, so his became the 'next' book.

Friday 31st July 1998

I come with love to my sister who writes the book with me and with Odette Churchill. I come to say how much we appreciate the work she is doing, the channelling she gives herself over to, the time she gives to the transcribing of the book for us both. For it is a story of great sadness and will be extremely difficult to write later on, but Sister knows this and will work through it, no matter what.

I also want to say to all who sit in the circle of light, thank you for accepting Daniel, for talking to him, for giving him your strength, your warmth and in some cases, your love.

Our sister knows she is a good channel and her longing to become totally clairvoyant has been heard and accepted by those in the realms. She is already aware of

Spirit around her and can almost see, soon she will see clearly and hear clearly.

Sister, I am come to tell you this now for you have asked many times for this to be. We have had to wait until you were ready and you are almost ready now.

All you ask for, mostly anyway, with regard to healing has been heard and will be answered. Not all, for some have their time of passing, as you know, but we can ease their passing if you ask.

Your own health is at risk and you need to rest. Your thoughts for tomorrow when you go to collect the beautiful lady are right; you need to wander, to sit, to photograph and to rest.

This has not been as easy as the book! For these are thoughts and this is in a work situation where it is not as easy to reach you, although you felt and almost saw Daniel without any problems a few moments ago.

These words are for you, sister, with our love.

Before long Odette will come and talk to you herself, for we are close even now and she will work with me through you. And you can talk to her too, direct, and we will make the book the world will want to read and understand, and you will earn money which you need so much. And yes, we will have our minds set at rest by the writing of it. In that you are right, dear sister.

I will withdraw now, let you think on these words. If I can come tonight, I will. If not, remember I have been with you this day and every day, remember I am always with you and you are smiling more lately than you have been because Daniel is there.

In love and peace I leave you now.

***

I am aware that an author in spirit helps me with my writing, which is the reference Daniel makes in the following communication.

19th August 1998

It is I, Daniel, who has been pushing you tonight, dear sister, to speak to you. It was I who removed the introduction from the computer, as it was not what I wanted, sorry to give you so much work, but you need a spirit inspired introduction, not a physical earth one. I know you understood even as you searched last night through all the directories in your computer, what a box of tricks that is! You would type better if the nails were shorter, but if the nails were shorter they would not look half as good, so - leave them as they are. I love them.

Your work on the book so far has been just what we wanted and we appreciate very much the time you are giving to channelling it. We will not overload you with the book, we will leave you time to write your own because there is this guy here who is waiting for you to get going again. He said it's long overdue and has been moaning that we are taking up your time. I told him how important this book is and he said so is his, because you need money, dear sister, to live and his will earn you money. I think ours will too, but we will have to see. Only joking, I know who it is and we will leave you time and that's a promise.

Your request for me to link with you for clairvoyance has been heard and is accepted. It will be a pleasure to work with you, sister, for you understand Daniel oh so well. You will know Daniel even better when the book is done, for you will know his secrets, thoughts and fears, his memories and his longing for peace of mind.

Daniel leaves you to get on with your watering, your picture hanging and your nails, which need repainting before tomorrow night and the platform at Fledglings. We will try some clairvoyance tomorrow, sister, if you feel confident enough to try it. Sit quietly on the platform, try and tune in to one person in the congregation and we will see what happens.

You will sleep tonight, for I will be there to watch over you. Tonight I will be your doorkeeper.

***

The outburst contained in the following communication came after a prickly circle, when one of the sitters actually accused Daniel of being an entity because he brought laughter instead of serious philosophy. The first communication was written with such anger and hurt that it had to be deleted and we began all over again.

Daniel wanted me to give this communication to the two people concerned but our circle leader advised against it, knowing it might inflame passions even more and, in fact, the people left the circle of their own accord.

22nd August 1998

It is I, Daniel, who comes this afternoon, half in sorrow, half in anger. Was it not enough that one of your Circle sitters asked if I needed to move on? Now I am accused of being an entity!

Let me say clearly now through Sister's computer, I AM NOT AN ENTITY!

Oh ye of little faith and understanding! ANY guide who comes through circle is an advanced soul, very advanced, for we are not allowed to approach the earth plane unless we are developed enough to be able to make that contact! Think about things, before you make your statements. Think carefully and long. All souls who approach a circle of light have a specific reason to do so, they come with messages, with philosophy, with a reason to make contact. I had been searching for 50 years to find the right circle to accept me, not only because so many refused to accept a clown, but because

I sought the right person to write my book. I came carefully to this circle of light, tentatively sending out a light vibration until I was sure of the sitters, but I can tell you now I was always sure of my sister! But it would have been hard for her if the others had not accepted me.

Let me tell you very, very briefly about Sister. She is marked by spirit for service, she has guides and helpers around her she has never mentioned to you, nor will she. She has her North American Indians, you all do, but her main guides now, at this point in her development, are a German Jew and a Cardinal. But - we are only representing ourselves that way as that was our last reincarnation. We both go back many, many centuries of experiences and lives on this earth plane of yours. We are very advanced teachers. Sister knows this in her heart, nothing which is going on her screen at the moment is a surprise to her, for we wrote this out once, she and I, and then I wanted to change it all. I wanted to change it for there was much I said first time which is not for you to know. Because, you do not seem to want to understand.

Let me say this. All lives need balance and that means laughter as well as sorrow. Sister has more than her share of sorrow, has done more than her share of crying. She needs a clown around her. She delights in her clown. She loves her clown. Her love is all compassionate, all consuming, all enveloping. Daniel basks in that love and gives it back.

Let me say this. Sister lives her life open to spirit all the time. She draws on us and we draw on her. She seeks strength and we give it. She seeks comfort and we give it. She asks little in the great scheme of life except to be given the privilege to serve and this we grant her, willingly. Because she is open to us all the time, we surround her with guardian angels and guides. A grey wolf walks alongside her and sleeps on her bed at night. A North American Indian brave stalks her every footstep. And Thomas, her Cardinal, and I are always there as doorkeepers, as watchers, as friends and constant companions. Sister is ever guarded.

Would an entity give such comfort, such love, such encouragement, such upliftment? Would an entity write the book we are writing at the moment, one to bring ease of mind to thousands of people? Would an entity dare show its face in a circle that is protected by a doorkeeper and by guides? No entity would be that foolish nor would it be allowed access at any time, for you are all protected by the Light. I say this before I close this communication. If you cannot accept Daniel for what he is, so be it, but do not doubt my sister's sincerity or what she receives, for it comes from the highest source, the great white spirit which is love.

Daniel closes this communication. Thank you, Sister, for giving me this time. Sorry about the first one …

***

26th August 1998.

A communication was received from Cardinal Thomas Lindenwood, when I was (as usual) asking many questions and he came to answer some of them. In this section, Thomas is referring to that angry communication:

'Daniel is quieter now, he has come to understand that nothing will ever be perfect in this material life, there will always be doubters. Even those who try to block him. But Sister, you are there for him and will defend him to the death if necessary. He knows that and he loves you for it.'

***

Comments on the following communication:

36

I have studied the crystals and taken a Crystal Healing course, but whether I will ever get to study geology is another matter entirely … The 'beautiful lady' is my medium friend Hazel Butterworth.

27th August 1998

It is I, Daniel, who is coming close this afternoon, dear sister. Often I come to you at work, as you know, as well as at home. I have taken the beautiful lady's love into my heart and yours and I feel much better. Thomas has also helped me a lot. I am advanced, yes, capable of making communication but still a fragile soul seeking consolation, encouragement and above all love and support that you give me, dear sister, and I welcome it and return it to you.

Today I come to tell you not to worry about your health. Your blood pressure did soar this morning, but it is the heat, the tiredness to some degree and the unquiet mind at the moment. The stone you chose has brought it down a lot and you are oh so right with these stones! They have such power! May I suggest you take time out to walk on the beach occasionally and pick up stones, raw as they are, and later polish them yourself, for you will find or be given the machine to do it with. Some Saturdays, instead of returning to work, or this Sunday when you may well be free, go down to the beach for a while and collect some stones for yourself. You have discovered the secret of the pebbles, their intense power, their intense radiation of energy and healing. You will do much with these stones. Go back now and begin to study the crystal course you paid for, learn about the crystals, move on to the minerals, begin your geological studies, for you will make a fine geologist along with everything else. We welcome, we encourage, we delight in your desire for knowledge. Study, study, study! And yes, buy more stones, for there are many to choose from to give away. You are right, the light coloured ones for ladies: the dark ones for men. Every time.

We will write the book, too, you and I, for you are working well and it is going well. It is going as I wish it to. Odette will come soon, to say hello for herself. Remember you need quiet times, they are not happening as often as you planned, but it is getting better, you are getting better, you are letting go more.

Live for Spirit, dear sister, not for mankind at the moment. Let that come through your love for Spirit.

And remember, Daniel is with you always and always, your own clown. And your very dear friend.

***

The new booklet Daniel refers to in the following communication is the Circle of Light, a magazine which appeared for the first time in September 1998. The 'temple of light' was a church that was giving me many problems at that time.

15th September 1998

It is I, Daniel, who comes close, sister, after a space of time. It is good to be back with you, to know you are there, waiting for me. I have been for healing with those Higher Beings who understand our sorrows and our fears, with those who can see into our minds and understand our tears. I bring you a lighter, loving vibration for the love you have been sending me, for the healing you have been sending me. I am much better now, the bitterness is passed through and out of my being and I am at one with myself

You have been alone with your thoughts, dear Sister, and such troubled thoughts, so little sleep, so much I worry. Fear not. You know I am one of the guardians of the church, I will not let anything happen there that is not right for your temple of light. I and the other guardians have the situation well in hand. Those who need to go will go; those who need to come in will come in. None will be your doing or that of the man you work with; it will all be the work of Spirit. The dear lady was right in that I needed healing, she was right to stir everything up for it cast great lights on that which needed to be lit and showed up the flaws in the structure of the people who build the church. She has now gone and will not return. New people will come; new friends of the church, to bring a different enlightenment to the people you all serve.

The new booklet is also casting light on many things and is a joy for us to see. Remember you do not write it alone, any more than I write my book by myself, I have my friends; you have your friends. Your stuffy Cardinal is here, he has been waiting patiently for your life to quieten down so that he can come back in again and talk to you of oh so serious things. I come still with laughter to uplift you and encourage you and lighten you. We have Fledglings again this week, as you call it, that odd time when learners get together and practice. You made great strides last time, Sister, and have done nothing since. So I will encourage you there to do more this week, to make another step forward and then another until you and I are as one to work together for the church you love.

Your Daniel is back, with love, with laughter, with joy and with happiness that the bad times are gone and the good times are ahead. We will still write the book, sister, for it needs to be written, there is much to be said. But in your time, when you are able. We will not push you in that we will only push you in your serving Spirit in the way you know will come.

I love you too, dear Sister.

Chapter 4

The problems did not go away, as Daniel mentions in this next communication.

30th September 1998

It is I, Daniel, who comes close to you this night, sister. It has been a while since we worked on the book but we, you and I, will get back to it and that is a promise. You have been distracted by a hundred different things, some hurtful, some draining, some difficult, always the tiredness and always the demands of the material life. But we will progress for there is much to be done and time, although it does not matter, is still running away from us.

Odette says hello.

Sister, do not worry so much about the temple of light. It will be all sorted out for you in the fullness of time. We wish you to live your material life with as much comfort and happiness as can be arranged in this time of your life, so yes, plan your garden of colour and beauty, give yourself something to do in the evenings when there is sunshine and when there is time to be at peace among the plants. Even in so small a space you can find peace.

Everything you are doing, from sending books to people to reading the books that arrive in your hands is what we want you to do. Your medium was right, you are surrounded by guides, so many loving people. Daniel is just one of them, but a close and loving one, as you know.

Sister, we will be with you when you journey. Your car will be full of those who love you. Sister, when you are moved to look at my portrait I am with you. Remember we are always, always around, ready to listen, ready to help. Open your heart and mind to us and let us guide you.

And let us give you the peace you so desire.

***

The nail and the cigarette mentioned in this next communication need to be explained.   A single false bright red fingernail was found at the bottom of a flight of stairs in the office suite we used. That week there had been no female visitors and the three women who worked there did not use false fingernails ... the cigarette, a 'tailor-made' was found on the stairs. Everyone who smoked at work at that time rolled their own ... but at least one work-mate said, 'it's something to do with your spooky friends, isn't it?'

18th November 1998:

'Daniel said he is sorry time is not with you at the moment to go on with the book but time will be there and you will write steadily in a while.'

6th January 1999:

After a very traumatic period of strife within the Spiritualist   movement;   a   lengthy   personal communication from Cardinal Thomas Lindenwood says: 'Daniel can come close now you are slowly letting go and the work can begin again on his book.'

***

You will see that the problems had continued but we were about to step down and leave it all.

15th January 1999

It is I, Daniel, who comes close this night, Sister. I have been around you all the time, but not able to come

41

close, because of the many problems you have had with grief, suffering and sadness all around you. Daniel cannot cope with other people's sadness; he has enough of his own. You always understand; you are someone who does understand many things. Some comes from your own self, some comes from spirit. I have to say the piece you wrote for your lovely magazine this afternoon was exactly right, you are the sort of person who needs to be open to spirit all the time. And we in turn love you for it.

I have been around you and your friends, trying to support and help and guide them. I have come to add my words to those of the other guides: you are doing the right thing. We are guardians of the church, we will not let any harm come to it, but for the time being it is right that you stand aside and let others do some work, to let them see how hard it is, how complicated it is, what effort you have all given to keeping it running all this time. They will not appreciate it until they do it for themselves. Let it go. Let go, as your Cardinal says so many times. Let go. It is harming your health, the headaches are not good for you. How much better you have been since you made the decision to leave! How much easier it has been for you to cope, knowing there is an end to it all.

And yes, the nail and the cigarette were my jokes. You knew that and the one who works with you, has an idea, doesn't he?

Soon you will be calm enough for us to start work again on the book. Soon the unhappiness in your heart will melt away like the snows of Potsdam with the coming of Spring and you and I will work on again. There is no rush; we can take our time. It will be a fine book when it is done. Allow yourself time, sister, time to be yourself. There are problems ahead, you know that already and you need to be strong to face up to them. I will be with you all the time, as will Thomas, Grey Bear and all the others around you, for you are much loved, much cared for, much protected, dear sister. We will let no harm come to you. We are working to bring you much happiness, in between the sad times, of which there are many ahead. But most of all, I come this night to tell you there will be much service for you to give, for you have the voice, the words, the confidence and the skills to bring the words to the people who need them. You and your friend will do much service for people, bringing comfort, philosophy, understanding and what I would call 'homespun' talks, straight out of your life, sister, and your heart. And Daniel will be there to support you and care for you and work with you.

Thank you for talking with me this night. I will not leave you again. I will learn to live through the sadnesses with you in future, so I do not leave your side ever again.

***

May 1999

This particular time was the aftermath of a very draining and exhausting period of business life encompassing all manner of problems. Meantime, our Circle leader had suffered a sort of breakdown, which always upset Daniel. My friend was moved to give me his portrait of Daniel, for the reasons Daniel gives.

Saturday 15th May 1999

It is I, Daniel, who comes to you this afternoon, dear sister. For too long we have been apart, while you have struggled with adversities and problems, with emotions and sadnesses but now it is over, it is time indeed for you to begin your spiritual journey again, as you said earlier today. I was there, I heard!

But although we have been apart, you have not once forgotten me, have you? You have sought me, sent thoughts to me, sent love to me and I have felt it and

43

received it and been glad of it. Your Cardinal, Thomas, has been around, not to mention the others, trying to get you to write, to meditate, to sleep, to work, to realise they are there! How busy you have been and how busy they would have you be!

At last, this day I can say the past is behind you, it is time to move on and your moving on will be interesting.

I asked to come to you, Sister, picture and all, for the sadness which lingers around your friend, my brother, is sometimes too much for me to handle. You are stronger, you are very feminine and cry easily but beneath the tears is the strong lady who can stand anything, who will stand anything, and endure. That is what I need.

We still have a book to write, my Sister! It will be done, it will very much be done, for Odette is here to say that to you through me. She wishes it to be written as much as I do. As soon as you get the computer box of magic tricks sorted, we will start again on the book, get something written at least two or three times a week and watch it progress.

Your garden grows under your loving hands, the plants flourish, there is beauty there and a haven for birds. I find you a haven for my easing of mind, in that you are the sort of person others go to for comfort. I came to you for comfort at the beginning, through your circle and so have stayed to draw it from you and to give it back, for you in turn have needed your comforting. Spirit has not let you down, and will not let you down. We are here, we are always here.

Sister, thank you for sparing the time this afternoon, for feeling my fingers in your hair, for being aware of me once again. We will work, I promise, and we will build a whole new relationship, you and I, for through me your clairvoyance will truly grow.

Daniel withdraws from this communication but not from the sister he loves. God bless and keep you, my dear.

***

1st July 1999:
Cardinal Thomas Lindenwood: 'Daniel is always around you – loving you and caring for you.'

***

My medium friend gave me a clown for Christmas, which Daniel mentions in this (abbreviated by me) communication.

16th January 2000
Tis I, sister, it is Daniel who has come to talk to you this afternoon. For too long I have been away from you, not far away, still watching and walking with you but not coming close, while you struggled with so many things. Your mind has been too full for me to come close, with the many problems you face on the earth plane. But now these problems are easing back, even if it doesn't feel like it, I can assure you it is happening, slowly.

It has been good to come close to you this afternoon. Thank you for the quiet time, thank you for the opportunity to speak. I am never far away, call on me when you need upliftment. I will do everything I can to make you laugh. Your clown is beautiful from the beautiful lady whom I love so much. Look at him and think of me and I will be there.

***

A visiting medium had said the new totally independent group my friend and I had started needed a focal point, a candle which should be lit at every meeting. So we bought one and I added two boxes of matches to ensure I could light it. But one Saturday the matches went missing from the carrier bag ...

16th May 2000

Sister, it is I, Daniel, who comes through your beautiful music tonight to come and speak with you, rather than impressing you with my thoughts for my story.

I come to apologise more than anything for we are not making very rapid progress with the book. I know at times you would like to write more but for me this is tremendously hard and that I know is something you also appreciate. I cannot write of these things without it tearing my heart out!

But we are making progress, slowly, we are past the first war, we are moving on, for a while our lives were relatively normal and we can write of that, and talk of that.

Believe me, I will finish this story! For you know, you have been told by so many now, it HAS to be written, it HAS to be said and it will sell. Your work, your devotion to me, will be repaid in the future, but I know that is not why you are writing it with me. You are doing it through and for love and no one has loved me this much for a lifetime of lifetimes.

Truly I gained so many friends when I came to your Circle that time! Even those who doubted me, who were unsure of me, they gave their love to me and encouraged me. Your dear friend who works so closely with you, he understands me so very well and knows of my great emotions. Your new friend, the one who saw me hiding from the troops, yes he too understands how hard it is for me to write this book.

But my dear Sister, we will, a page at a time, progress this terrible story of mine. I had such a bad life, such a traumatic life, that I cannot bring myself to return to the earth plane for another life for fear of it being as bad. I must make my progress through the realms as best I can. First I must unburden myself of the guilt, the fears, the sadness and the intense loneliness that my life brought me. I am slowly doing that, through you.

It would be hard for me to find the right words to thank you for your devotion to Daniel so I will not try. I will only say I walk with you and always will. I will protect you and always will. I will love you and always will.

And yes, I did take the matches ...

***

28th May 2000

'The clearing out process you have been through has settled your mind considerably. It has also given you proof – for the likeness of our friend Daniel which you found in your own work so resembles that drawn by your circle sitter that you can no longer doubt yourself. But we agree, you will never be a psychic artist! That is something you have to let go. You are not sorry to let it go, we know that.' (Thomas was absolutely right, I cannot draw and never will be good enough, but I drew enough rough portraits to give myself all the proof I needed.)

***

31st May 2000

A communicator whom I think of as my 'Big Man' a protective strength giving guide, came through with a personal communication, which included this paragraph:

'Your young friend, Daniel, is finding it hard to write his book. I ask that you be patient with him even more as he tries to write his words. You know the book will be done eventually but meantime it is hard for him and you as well, channelling these traumatic words.

***

I was chairing for a very strong medium one Sunday, with all the usual butterflies that chairing brings. As the medium began his opening prayer, so I became aware of Daniel in his harlequin outfit sitting on the table by my side, swinging his legs, whispering "he's not half bad, is he?" which brought instant concealed giggles and a lessening of tension and nerves. This is something he likes to do: it lifts me immediately and helps – as he well knows.

***

My medium friend said she knew when Daniel was around her, for the 'Fiddler On The Roof' song comes into her mind. She suggested I ask Daniel for a song to tell me when he is around, which I did. Had I given it any thought, I would have come up with the song myself, the one he took all of five seconds to find for me – "Tears Of A Clown." Not that I need a song, I *know* when he is there.

***

10th August 2000

It is I, Daniel, who comes to put aside the book for a moment, dear Sister, for we reach a most traumatic moment again and I have to build my heart up to face it. We will, and soon, we will push the book forward.

My reason for coming tonight is to thank you for all the love. Thank you for asking me for a sign that I am coming near to you and it is with fun in my heart that I give you that sign. I draw close to you tonight for once again the pain is in the head and you are not happy with yourself at all.

I know you are weighed down with worries and sadnesses, but you know that in the course of life there must be partings and passings and problems and you know this. We will see you through, we will be there with you, our hands on yours, our arms through yours, holding and helping and guiding.

***

This next communication came through just before Daniel was about to start on the real horror story of his life – his arrest and transportation to the concentration camp. This was when the book began to get seriously hard to write, as if it had not been difficult enough before –

12th October 2000
This is Odette.

I come to say thank you for the love, the help, the understanding and the devotion you offer to Daniel and myself.

This will not be a long communication for I am new to this but must learn to speak with you in this way so we can write the book.

You are right, in the 'reading' so long back, I appeared in the green and gold dress and said I would help you with the next book. This is the next book.

We are moving into a part of the book now that will tear Daniel apart in the telling but which will heal his soul when it is told. Be patient, sister, be loving and be there. We both need you.

***

Around this time the song changed, the one by which I was to know Daniel was around. I have to say that he hardly ever used "Tears Of A Clown" anyway, perhaps it was the title he needed to give more than the song itself. *(He just said yes)*. I found myself waking up with two lines of an old Burl Ives song in my head: "A little bitty tear let me down/spoiled my act as a clown."

***

24th October 2000

It is I, Daniel, who asks for this time to write to my sister. You are wise to use the music to distract yourself from my words, for that is the only way you could possibly cope with the words which are going into the book at this time. I feel strong right now, I feel able to cope, for we have broken a sort of barrier by working like this, by your pushing me just a little last week to make another effort. I feel now we will make rapid progress.

You did so make me laugh last week when you handed me your handkerchief! It was at that point I knew I had to be strong and write the book for you and for me, for there is no point in my dissolving into tears and stopping all the time, much as I long to!

Odette is here, she is comforting me, she is giving me her strength from this side even as you give me your strength from that side. With two such ladies, how can I not make the book a success, in that it will tell the truth of what went on and who was involved and the world must realise and remember that, time may have gone by but there are many, here and with you on the earth plane, who still suffer from the effects of that terrible time all those years ago. For there is no time in the realms and so we suffer as if it were yesterday.

50

And the story must be told to answer those who say it never happened.

We made progress tonight. Good progress. We will make even more progress tomorrow and you will take your time out on Thursday to rest and to sit Circle and to receive the calm and serenity which communion with the spirit world gives you. And then we will do more on Friday and so we will progress until the book is finally done.

My love to you for all you have done and for all you will do for me. I would like my communications from Circle to be included, tell your friend to find them for you, for it will take some time to transcribe my words. They will then be included in the book and so we will have a book which will surprise those who do not understand and interest those who do. And we will have no names in the book, apart from mine and Odette's, so they cannot pester and bother those who love Daniel so much. No earth plane names. We will keep them away from the prying eyes of those who do not understand.

My love, always.

Chapter 5

The book was progressing steadily, we covered much ground, most of it heartbreakingly sad. Then Daniel visited us in a very small home circle, only four of us sitting in a peaceful flat in Sandown. For some reason, before we settled to our meditation, I began to talk of the book, of Daniel and his closeness, of his need to get the book done. There was so much I had not told people about his life, as I wanted them to read it for themselves. In particular, I had made a point of not telling anyone anything about his childhood and the tragedies in his family. Daniel came through my friend Brian that night; here is a transcript of the communication we received.

***

26th October 2000

Daniel - You have been talking of me and I have been very close to you. The first communication was on October 27th 1997. You asked me for this, my sister.

Dorothy -Yes I did.

Daniel - I am still a little sad for it is churning, all that happened during my life on earth the last reincarnation which took in the last World War when I, Daniel, was a prisoner of war within the German concentration camps. For there was one that I spent the majority of my time in and on the two occasions that I managed to escape I was recaptured on both occasions and for a while taken to a different camp. I had told you this before and I have come to terms with my life through your help. For it is for people to be able to read about the accounts of Daniel's life and others in those prisoner of war camps. When I come to speak I am not quite so full up with emotion for through circles such as yours and the beautiful lady who is a very good communicator between the two worlds whom you know, because this is the Daniel that shows himself to you when dressed as a clown. I have been helped.

Dorothy -Yes.

Daniel - For there are two sides to Daniel. Yes and it is very difficult for you to relate to this in book form but it is my way of trying to erase all that happened to me and others whilst in the prisoner of war camps, so how I was on earth is how it must be told and you have been very patient for still I cannot give you the words as quickly as I, Daniel, would like to because when going back through my childhood which was horrific and only you know that, my sister.

Dorothy –Yes.

Daniel - Not even the one I speak through have I mentioned anything about an horrific childhood but you know I was badly treated, beaten at times. You have been very kind to Daniel but all must be revealed.

Dorothy - You have not mentioned that so far.

Daniel - That is to come for there is a twist.

Dorothy – Right.

Daniel - For my father was very sadistic to me, we have not got that far, you understand.

Dorothy - This is something you will reveal later.

Daniel - I will say to you that when I, Daniel, had to go through – I am sorry …

Dorothy - Take your time, we have the time –

Daniel - It was not until I was in the prisoner of war camp that I found out my father's true identity. You understand now why it is so difficult for me.

Dorothy - Yes I do.

Daniel - There will be a friend, a friend who is close to you, was poorly educated whilst on the earth but did very well for himself in the field of politics and he is going to help I, Daniel, to speed the process up for you to make it easier for you and me. He will give me that help and that guidance and that is why he also has come into the framework of your work with the spirit world.

Dorothy – Yes.

Daniel- You know this gentleman?

Dorothy - Yes I do.

Daniel - You know why.

Dorothy – Yes.

Daniel - It does not matter for I, Daniel, to say it. Because it concerns Odette.

Dorothy - Yes it does.

Daniel - That is the link.

Dorothy - You need the strength.

Daniel - We both need his strength for I was tortured but you all know what happened to Odette, don't you? It is very touching for Daniel and it is for you also but when I first was able to make communication with you, you were thinking within the framework of your minds that my first communication with you was three years ago almost to the day and I have come and spoken perhaps on a handful of occasions, no more. For I belong with the lovely lady that I joke and play around with for she has told you the naughty things that I, Daniel, do when with her. But communications that I had with you and her are almost word for word and you have had proof of this.

Dorothy – Yes.

Daniel - That is why I, Daniel, have chosen my contacts on the earth very carefully for I need to trust. The lady sat with you tonight has a beautiful nature, is a very thoughtful and understanding lady who has had many upsets and disillusionments throughout her life and she knows also how Daniel feels.

On the third occasion that I had escaped I was shot. I thought that I was going to escape and be free for I had got a little further than on the previous two occasions, there was quite an expanse of water to travel across in a

54

small rowing type of boat; that was not difficult but it was as I came out of the forests and into open land that I and many others were mowed down. I find it a little easier to speak of my experiences but when it comes to relating them for the book, then the emotions take me over and this is why the one so close to Odette Churchill and myself, Daniel, will speed completion of all facts that need to go into the book, and Daniel thanks you.

Dorothy - I consider it an honour to do the work.

Daniel - Daniel just wants to say thank you, for if it was not for that first communication then the book would not have been possible and also Daniel would still have been earthbound but through your kindness, all your kindness in those circle conditions and light you were able to move Daniel further along the path of progression and I now can come and speak to you and then go and return under happier conditions and that is my aim.

I wish to leave behind the uniform of the convict for that was what it was like in the prisoner of war camp. That was hell in a white and black spotted type uniform. But Daniel much prefers to be dressed as a joker and if I have to move things you will always find them.   I do apologise to the channel I speak through and his devoted lady who has had many problems this year but through all of us that work closely with her from the spirit world, Daniel included, for the love she showed me, she has come through with flying colours but I must apologise to both for taking a whistle and depositing it somewhere else for someone else to return it. May I laugh?

Circle sitter - Please do.

Daniel - Because you know it to be true.

Circle sitter – Yes.

Daniel - And it shows you that the world of spirit are so close to you. They say that I was 27 when I was shot and killed by the Germans. But Daniel's age was 35. But I will endeavour to concentrate and work much harder with the one who will give me great strength to complete the book as soon as possible because we don't wish to drain the one who has to listen and put it down on paper. So you will see a much more confident Daniel because the quicker it is finished the better for us all.

Odette was never the same after the war. It was something she had to live with; for Daniel it was something I had to live with but had to return to find those on the earth that could put my words for others to read, for my karma had to be sorted on the earth but due to what happened to me I was not strong enough to come back and face another material life upon earth but the earthly karma still had to be sorted and that was the only way that I, Daniel, could see it through.

Dorothy – Yes.

Daniel - You were talking for a time this evening. I heard you speak of Daniel, I was here and I was listening. It was peaceful and it's been warm and before I came through to speak to you, did you hear the aircraft?

Circle sitter - Yes.

Daniel - Thank you. Daniel leaves you. I am not sad, I leave you happy.

Circle sitter - Good. That's good.

Daniel - You were meant to speak about Daniel.

Dorothy – Yes.

Daniel - And as time goes on and we have the book, we will call it 'the wretched book'; as far as Daniel is concerned, taken away then I can come more frequently and speak to you.

Dorothy - That will be lovely.

Daniel - Daniel leaves you. I have tears because you are so kind. I am not going to say any more but I will just leave you with my love and my protection.

Dorothy - Thank you.

Daniel -For all of you and just to say to you all once more, for all those that touched Daniel's life, thank you.

56

And I freely confess to the reader that after Daniel withdrew that night, I sat and simply cried.

30th October 2000

It is I, Daniel, who wishes to talk without putting words into the book this night, sister. Your tears moved me very much last week when I spoke with you at Circle. Your tears were freely given, as your love is. Now you begin to see where your service to Spirit is going. Yes, you will be clairvoyant, for that is your wish and it will be good to work with you, when I can shed my convict outfit and become your court jester, your harlequin, your clown. Then the clairvoyance will be such fun, my sister! But outside of that, I will be bringing people to you to hear their stories, perhaps to relate their stories, to put them into a book as well, a book of sadness with the message that there is life eternal, for the stories will come from this side and not from your side.

And in doing this, as the beautiful lady said, you will release others who are earthbound at the moment.

And in doing this, the service you do will be incalculable, my sister.

I will come again to talk you when the need is great, when we need to talk face to face about the book, and if you cry again, my sister, I am sorry but your need will be as great to release the emotion as mine is. I will come to talk through you from time to time as well, to prove to others that it can be done and that your soul is mine, for we share so much. You have kept so much back from the book so far that others will have to read, for even in the telling of it I sense your hurt, so you do not talk about it very much. This is good in some ways, but bad in others, for you store up the emotions. So perhaps I need to make you cry, to release it all, do you agree?

But your tears moved me deeply, for no one has cried for Daniel, ever, until you did that the other night. I am still in a state of shock that you feel so deeply, although I knew – of course – how much you care for me. The tears showed me the depth of love and it is great, it is deep, it is all encompassing. I can live with such a love. I can be released from sadness with such a love.

How can I thank you for that love?

How can I thank you for writing the book for me?

I will devote my time to serving you, being your guide, being your clairvoyant guide and we will make it fun, you and I, we will make them laugh as does the beautiful lady, for laughter is needed. You need it.

I will return your love a thousand-fold, Sister, you will never be alone.

***

Daniel came through at circle the following week, a different circle, but equally trusted sitters. I had been used that evening by a new communicator, one who had asked me if I would allow myself to be used in a one to one conversation some weeks before. I had been waiting for him to make use of me and he did for the first time that night. I can only assume Daniel felt we needed to talk again about the book and certainly to give me and the other sitters some upliftment.

To clarify one point, I received a telephone call from Hazel, (the beautiful lady) to say she had 'lost' her Coptic cross and would I ask 'him' to give it back to her. She found it three months later, in a vase in the bottom of her wardrobe... this is the reason for the conversation I had with Daniel at that time concerning 'her cross.'

3rd November 2000

It is I, Daniel, I have stood back in order for the new communicator to move aside in order to allow the channel to be free and to be protected and to say thank you from the realms and for those of you on the earth for the communication from the new communicator whose name and identity will be given to you when the time is right.

Daniel has been here from the beginning, has had tears but most of you know Daniel's problems dating back to the prisoner of war camp. I did have tears but this evening I have been able to shed those tears. A most unusual evening, most unusual, unusual music but has made Daniel happy. Probably not all of you like it but if Daniel knew the words, he would sing to you but I do not know the words. Do any of you know the words? Speak to Daniel.

(Sitters spoke).

You must have been inspired to put that on because it has made me happy and a new communicator has come through so nothing has been lost, has it? The music the chanting, it has blended in with the fireworks. It is interesting to see at the moment in your particular part of the world so many people are stockpiling with petrol; maybe it is a form of a gunpowder plot to blow up your government. All governments are useless. Do you not agree?

I have come in a much happier way but then I have been playing with the beautiful lady today. She will tell you, the one who is writing Daniel's book, she will tell you what I have done. I have been mischievous.

Dorothy - Did you give back her cross?

Daniel - No.

Dorothy - You said you would.

Daniel - She must ask me nicely, she must ask me nicely and then I will give her what she wants that belongs to her. I have not taken it, I have hidden it. The channel I speak through, for 18 months has been looking, hunting for the communication from Daniel, the first one. Could not find it. He opens the folder and there it is. Daniel took it for a while but placed it back. I always return things.

Dorothy - When is that?

Daniel - When I am ready. But you are also coming very close on the earth to what you know as Remembrance Sunday and this at the moment does not make Daniel sad because it is a time for all of you to associate with what Remembrance Sunday is about, not just the past World Wars, more recent confrontations like the Falklands, but your loved ones who have passed and are now in the spirit world who at this time come close to you to remember, to remember all those great people, some not so great, who fought in the wars through various confrontations battles fought abroad but involving your nationality, my nationality, for I was a German Jew as you all know but I was treated very badly and still Germany is still treating people, nations, they have not learned. For one thing that has upset Daniel recently is when your country was called upon to help out with the situation that was very deep in the hearts of the decent Germans when a submarine was lost at sea and nothing was done by this nation: they left them to perish and yet many, many weeks later through your world's newspapers, through the media a note was found that many were still alive and yet perished because nothing was done. It is so sad.

But then I Daniel and thousands and thousands perished within the prisoner of war camps, your country other countries were fighting but still we have the anger and the jealousy and the hatred between people, races, nations throughout your world. Only when you can live in peace in love and in harmony with each other can you progress towards a world of love and light and it is as your fields where those lost their lives are surrounded, covered with poppies to remember those that gave their lives for their country, not just your country, my country as well, because there were good Germans but just send your thoughts out to all those who have fought for their countries through the decades, through the various confrontations for they did so believing that in the end peace would surround your world. But still in the biblical countries you still have this fighting, this hatred, this greed, all for what? The wealth of nations. Everything needs to be balanced out.

This is strange for I, Daniel, said that I would not give any form of philosophy but I am coming to terms with my karma. It is true that karma, cause and effect, must be sorted whilst upon the earth, it cannot be sorted in the realms for I, Daniel, have found it very difficult because through my life, my problems, this reincarnation on earth I have not been able to move away from the pull of the earth because of what happened to me, not just within the prisoner of war camp but my early childhood which was horrific, and as I come to terms with all that has happened, I can now go forward and give the information, the proof that is needed to the one who has sat so patiently for just a few sentences at times. For I am now ready. My voice through the channel I speak through is much stronger, I feel much confidence, much more confident, for the lady I have been associated with for a long time, the one you know I call the beautiful lady, the very first communication that I gave to the channel I speak through I also gave to her, word for word, and they have compared the communications which is proof of Daniel's identity.

So just remember all those who have passed. Those who were in prison in the prisoner of war camps, those who died in those camps for they all played a part in order for you to be living the lives you have here today. The standard of living has improved but in some cases it has gone over the top for so many because still the rich have got richer and the poor have got poorer. So wealth must be evenly distributed and in time this will happen.

You have so much beauty around. Your climate is changing but then it has since the beginning of time and in the beginning homes were built on stony ground and on marshy areas - nothing has changed. You do not listen. You do not take notice.

When you play the music again, Daniel will return. It is not my kind of music but I am growing to it and it does uplift me.

Have you gone to sleep, all of you? No? Are you bored?

Dorothy – No!

Daniel - Wipe away your tears for I have your tears as well as mine.

Dorothy – It has been a bit heavy.

Daniel – Times have been heavy but I am coming out of those times for you have all helped me and as the first communicator said, in a way you must let all your burdens go because at the end of life's day whatever happens, whether it be good or bad, you cannot change what has happened and nor can Daniel. And so that has helped as well. Who has had a headache today?

Dorothy - I have.

Daniel - I had to say that to you because I wanted to draw close but I knew you were going to be busy this evening and occupied within your meeting but we will give it 2-3 days and we will have a purge. Do you understand the word purge?

Dorothy – Yes.

Daniel - It won't be heavy. What has got to be written will be on the heavy side but Daniel will come through as he has tonight and it will make it easier.

Dorothy - We have made tremendous progress.

Daniel - We are improving but we don't have to tell them that, do we? It is between you and me and it is a secret and it will be nice when you can say the book is completed and it won't be too long now for I have the help of Odette.

Dorothy - She is a lovely soul.

Daniel - She was when on the earth and what she went through was horrific. She lived for a while to tell the tale but she could never erase that from her mind. And so through the book it will also help her to come to terms with what happened to her, which is very touching. It will be a tear-jerker but all the truths have to be told.

Dorothy – Yes.

Daniel - For there is so much that people did not know about for the information has not only come from Daniel but there is a part, very important part, for Odette and you realise this now.

Dorothy – Yes. I came across a text the other day – 'ye shall know the truth and the truth shall set you free.'

Daniel - There is nothing more to say for the words speak for themselves. If you will just sit quietly, my friends, and just imagine all the poppies falling down from the skies. What you imagine to be poppies will be real for the red poppies falling from the skies from the realms, you will see those poppies falling and forming into a Christmas tree, for you are also drawing close to the festive season. Enjoy, be happy, for once Daniel is going to enjoy Christmas.

Dorothy - That will be wonderful.

Daniel - For there was not one Christmas that Daniel could enjoy in the last reincarnation upon the earth so think of the red poppies falling as a Christmas tree for your upliftment, for your protection and to say thank you.

Symbolically together we will place a Christmas tree covered with red poppies at where I was held in the concentration camp not far from a place you now know as Dortmund and that tree, laden with poppies, are for all of Daniel's friends who lost their lives at that camp. Peace be with you.

Dorothy - And with you, dear friend

Daniel - Shall we sing before Daniel goes? Would do, but do not know the words. My joke. We could dance - shall we dance?

Dorothy - Perhaps not this time.

Daniel - Obviously not. The gentlemen could dance - probably not. The lady to the channel's left could dance - probably not – It's no good Daniel dancing by himself, is it?

Daniel leaves you with love and protection.

I must return to the beautiful lady and I will give her back what she's asked me for.

Telephone her if you like tonight, it will be there.

Daniel leaves you.

Chapter 6

A dear friend passed unexpectedly to the Summerlands. This communication came through from Daniel.

29th November 2000

Sister, it is I, Daniel, who wishes to come to you tonight outside the book, to talk with you alone, one to one.

Your sorrow is intense, as much for the others as for yourself. Being sensitive you have picked it all up and carry the burdens of them all. I have been with you all day, I was there with the little frightened sorrowing lady – but you knew that, you heard the footsteps and heard the television crackle and the noises from behind – I was there and I was working with you to raise a smile occasionally and you did, sister. You did very well.

Some Spiritualists believe it is wrong to grieve, knowing that the soul has gone home to the Summerlands but it is not wrong to grieve, for you are desperately missing the human presence and that is hard. Very hard. It takes a while to get used to the idea the person physically is not around anymore, but that their spirit is and you are wise not to mention it to anyone but your dear man. He heard you, he absorbed what you said, but he too is in shock and denial, as his partner is. But what you said will linger in his mind and will comfort when nights are long and the sadness comes walking.

Whatever happens, you know you have your loving Daniel there now, all the time, for courage, strength, support and encouragement. Yes, there is a reason why that soul was called home and in a short time you will know why.

Odette and I wish to thank you for the work on the book, which has been wonderful. Your devotion is beyond price. The truth is, you do it for love and not for reward and that is the difference.

You asked if my part of the book will be done by Christmas, yes it will. This is why I said it will be a happy Christmas for me for the first time ever. To do that we must do a lot of work, sister, but you are ready, willing and capable, despite your sorrow and headaches. And I will come and talk with you again, one to one, through your own fingers and through your channelling friend, very soon.

Meantime, if you wish, we will return to the book and do a little more this night. My dear sister, my heart grieves with you but believe me, it was meant to be. Nothing is by chance. It was right at that time, in that place, for many reasons which Spirit could not explain to you if they tried, for the plan is vast and the intricacies complex. Believe, trust and have faith. It was meant and it will be right in time for many people.

Sister, you have my love. Always.

***

Should anyone ever have a single doubt about the workings of Spirit, I will take just a moment here to say that the friend in question passed immediately after a bypass operation, whilst in Intensive Care. We were told later that he was a walking time bomb: he could have passed anywhere, any time. So we are consoled, for he did not crash his car and take someone else with him, fall down in his home or at work or in the street, but passed with dignity and in peace, not knowing of his physical passing. Spirit's plan is nothing but a series of gentle miracles.

Believe, trust and have faith – true words, for all does become clear in the fullness of time and the miracle is revealed.

I have included this communication to make the point to Spiritualists that it is all right to grieve, to non-Spiritualists that there are reasons for everything and to prove to Daniel that he is indeed a philosopher, though he always vowed he would never bring philosophy through …

***

19th December 2000

Good evening, Sister. It is Odette who is with you, as you have already realised. It is good that you know who it is who comes to you.

I come to offer you thanks for the work you have done and the work that is still left to do. Does that sound silly? The book is almost completed, Daniel's part is done, he has no other words to add now, but you need to add his words from the tapes which your friend has of the times when Daniel visited your Circle. It will make the first part of the book a true record of a relationship/friendship which has developed along lines you never thought it would but which Daniel planned it would from the very first. How grateful we both are that you gave us your time, your energy, your commitment, your love to this daunting project. We are also grateful for your confidentiality, you speak of the book without giving away any of its twists and turns, any of its really deep and tormented sections and yet you have aroused enough interest already for people to want the book to be published. Such is the skill you bring to your marketing!

Fifty years is a long time to carry a burden and now it has been put down. The clown has come into his own, he is happy at last. No matter what happens to you over this Christmas period – and there might be many things which will bother, disturb and move you at times – you will know you made him very happy and even if you feel sad, as you do right now, he is happy and that happiness is off-setting your own feelings because happiness is catching.

I too feel as if a burden has been laid down. He wrote of me with truth and delicacy, it is hard to convey a relationship between two people in a horror camp like that, when one refuses to speak but I can tell you that Daniel was a lifeline for me, despite his non speaking, or maybe because of it. He had no need of words at that time, he has an expressive face which says everything. He was and is my most trusted friend.

I am glad to say that now you are a trusted friend too, dear sister. Your light editing touch, your attention to detail has helped Daniel, for a story as emotive as his often wound back on itself, or statements were made which were later contradicted, how gently you altered them and how carefully you kept to the sense and feeling of his words.

We are almost there. We are almost at the point when you too can say 'it is done' and relax and consider other projects, other writing. There is the work on the Ramadhan lectures, as you have said, there are the poems of Ramadhan's channel to be typed, there is no end to the work everyone has to do when they take up the path of Spiritualism and take on the mantle of service to Spirit but you love the work, you are fulfilled by the work, which is why you were chosen.

I leave you this night with our thanks, with our love and with our protection.

Odette.

***

As Odette mentioned, I have been scanning and working on the lectures of the great teacher Ramadhan.

In one I came across a section that might answer some of the questions regarding Daniel's incarnation. For certainly it seemed to have gone 'wrong' in that there was just so much tragedy and heartache to carry that it almost proved too much to bear.

'Q. When we reincarnate, do we have the choice of our parents, country and race, or do we just take 'pot luck'?

A. Most of the people who come into a meeting of this nature are those who have come again into the mortal experience, bringing with them some lingering memory of the long-distant past. Such ones, having had a previous experience and wishing to come again into the mortal life for some special purpose, will be taken to what can only be described as the Great Place of Viewing, wherein they may be enabled to look into the aura of your earthly world to see there some of the coming events, such as the coming of wars or famines. Then they will be shown events in certain lands, and if they have some especial desire or work they wish to accomplish, then will they be shown the particular land, the opportunities, or the lack of opportunities, which will be there; eventually they will be helped to choose those who will be their parents who will best fulfil their purpose, or to help develop their soul qualities. But sometimes a soul may choose simply to be born to a certain family because it is unable to reach those who would give it its own life experience and so it may come into a family condition in which there may be great difficulty, sometimes rejection, but because it has chosen this, so it has the strength to overcome the difficulties and to overcome the feelings of rejection that the parents or the family may give. And when I say that it comes for special reasons, it may come sometimes with the desire to serve, but very often with the wish to develop certain soul qualities of patience, understanding and wisdom.'

I have no way of knowing for sure that this is the answer. All I do know is, the life which is related in the second half of this book is one of unmitigated horror and sadness, overwhelming heartbreak and sadness. But as Daniel himself has said, it is a story which must be told.

So the second part of this book is devoted to Daniel himself and the story which he gave through me.

Part II - Life on Earth

Chapter 7

I was born on the 16th November in the early part of last century in Potsdam in Germany, the last child of David and Eva Goleznovitch. There were already three children living in the small flat above the pawnbroker's shop: David Junior, Rosa and Solomon. David was five years old when I arrived; Rosa and Solomon were three, the only twins in the family and a source of great interest to the relatives.

Of which there were many.

My earliest memories are of the small flat: just three rooms and crude toilet, those rooms endlessly crowded with loving aunts and uncles, grandparents in thick black coats trimmed with curly fur, of hats with flaps in the winter and yarmulkes for the men the rest of the time. Beards I remember, thick, curly, long, straggly, multi-coloured beards and the smell of kosher cooking and perfume mixed with the mustiness of clothing and footwear from the shop below. I remember too the loving embrace of the female relatives, of looking up into faces filled with love and kindness, of smiling eyes and smiling mouths, of cooing and daft words as any child hears for the first two years of their life.

I remember love.

I remember love with sadness, for the whole family was love, no one fought in front of the children, no one swore or even looked angry in front of the grandmothers, both revered ladies with corseted bodies and strict views on the behaviour of children.

I remember love with sadness for it is something I have sought ever since.

The male relatives were just as kind in a different way. They patiently spent time with a little one, showing me over and over how to tie a bow in a lace, how to button trousers and shirts, how to make something out of a piece of wire, infinite patience, infinite kindness, infinite love. Grandfather Moishe was my favourite, he of the longest whitest beard and kindest bluest eyes and wrinkly face and large squared off hands set with rings and a huge mole that always fascinated me. I would touch it with disgust and yet unrestrained curiosity and he would smile and say:

"Such intense concentration from the little one, Eva, one day he will be a scientist or a doctor, for sure."

But grandparents were always wishing the finest professions for the grandchildren: was not David Jnr about to become the finest lawyer Potsdam had ever seen, even though he was not yet ten? Was not Rosa a nurse of some kind and Solomon a doctor and they not yet done with running wild through the fields not so far from our street of tightly packed houses and shops, of roofs which leaned into one another as if having conversations about the strange people who lived beneath them.

For we were a strange, motley lot indeed! Father worked as a tailor, stitching the clothing for the fine men who came to order, to be measured, to choose the cloth and to choose the design of a fine suit to fit a fine expensive body. Poor Father with his poor eyesight and cheap reading glasses so he could see the thread in the needle's eye and the holes in the buttons to be stitched on tight, for no gentleman needed a button falling off his new expensive suit. Father would hunch all day over the aged sewing machine, watching the dark material slide by, held together by even darker thread, none of it doing his eyes any good. Poor Father, even now I think of him as Poor Father, so small, round shouldered from the hours of sitting behind the table or the machine, sewing,

sewing, sewing. He was a meek man, almost colourless, with a gentle smile and the quietest of voices.

And the man who owned the tailor's shop, the man who hired and worked to death those who would labour for him, the Russian immigrant, Ivan Ivanovitch, was loud and boorish and arrogant and demanding and Poor Father and the other poor wretches who needed the work, cowered under the weight of words thrown at them day after day from the large man with the huge body and even huger voice. I think Poor Father was even quieter than he would have naturally been, living and working under such a loud man made him that way.

He would come home with fingers raw from strong thread, from stabs with the needles, with an aching back and tired eyes from the machine and the dark cloth.

I ventured once into the shop where he worked, surrounded by rolls and rolls of dark cloth, some with stripes, some with patterns, most with darkness woven into it, saw the lantern hanging from the ceiling, the single light by which they all worked. I saw the men, cowed by the voice of the Russian who held their lives in his hands, for work was not plenty in the early 1900s for Jews who were immigrants; we might have been second generation German but we were immigrants for all that, for we could not trace a perfect German line back through our ancestors.

I do not know where we came from originally, perhaps even from England, for we had English names handed down to us through the family: were there not Aunts and Uncles Rosa, Solomon, David, Daniel? I do not know for I did not ask. I thought I was German, I thought myself a German Jew, living in a small town in Germany, a country which was my whole world.

I repeat, I saw the men cowed by the voice of the Russian. The men were all small, like my father, round shouldered, meek of face, quiet of voice, quick of fingers - and desperate for work. I smelled the smell of misfortune, of despair, of gratitude, of subservience and I hated it. I never went in the shop again. If Mother sent me to ask Father for something, I would stand at the doorway and call to Mr Ivanovitch that I needed to see my Father for a moment - and I would only keep him for a moment. It was a rare happening and Mr. Ivanovitch knew my Mother would not ask unless it was an emergency. One time it was when Rosa fell the entire flight of stairs and needed a doctor and she wanted to ask if we had the money - oh the thought of those burdens! Another time David was in a fight in school and Father was needed to talk to the teacher and sort it out, for it was a dangerous and difficult time.

For those who believe the problem with and for the Jews started in the Second World War, think again.

The tailor's shop was in a row of similar shops in our main street. Dark brooding buildings, they were, with overhanging balconies like huge eyebrows and the windows above like eyes, watching every move a child made. I was a fanciful child even then, living on Grimm's fairy tales and other myths and legends that filled my heart with delicious fluttering fear.

Two doors along from the tailor's was the milliners where Mother worked, stitching the pretty hats and scraps of silk and feathers women wore on their heads, for it was a time when no woman uncovered her head, especially if she was Jewish. There was a demand for scarves, for hats, for coverings of all kind. So Mother and Father worked two doors away from one another, but a million miles in difference! For Mother worked with light, colourful, pretty things: ribbon, silk, artificial flowers and that in turn reflected on the shop itself, which was lighter, more welcoming, more encouraging, for ladies needed coaching, enticement, incentives to come and buy, where the men just bought dark dour suits to cover their bodies and look respectably dull at the synagogue. Here we were welcome, provided we did not touch and Frau Heinemann would smile at us - for Rosa was often with me, she being enchanted by the colour, the styles, the scraps of silk and feathers - and offer us dark tea and hard biscuits.

Other ladies worked there, only two or three, the number changing as the shop's fortunes fluctuated: Fraulein Himlin, a big lady with tight clothes and rolls of fat but motherly and ever welcoming, (Mother would often wonder aloud to Father why she had never married, suspecting some romantic tragedy in the past and embroidering it in her mind), Frau Bittenhau, a small lady with sharp eyes, sharp nose and chin, a model for all the witches in all the fairy tales I learned to read, and Frau Kleinser, who never seemed to stop laughing. It was Frau Bittenhau who lost the job when times were hard but somehow was always asked back when things were good again. Mother was so quiet, so good at her work, so inventive with her styles and her ability to make a hat look just that little bit different from the one she had just made that Frau Heinemann would never let her go.

Mother. The word alone brings tears and a lump I cannot bear. So beautiful a lady, in body and in soul. Pale face with the gentlest of smiles, pale hands with the gentlest of touches, could I say a pale voice for it was gentleness itself, ever soothing, ever there. She was golden haired, my mother, the beautiful gold she passed on to me, for all the other siblings were dark of hair and dark of eye. I was always the different one, from birth, through the life I had ahead of me. And it was this very difference which made a clown of me, for to clown, to tumble, to joke, to laugh, to play tricks, meant attention getting and I was ever in competition with those very siblings, they being older and more intelligent than I, they being first and second born, and how grandparents dote on the firstborn grandchild! The last, although loved, is and always will be the last.

Memories.

Hot days in summer when the dust rose choking around the cluttered clustered houses and shops, when the rooms were like ovens and we could hardly breathe for the thickness of the air. Father and Mother at work, David supervising us younger ones, keeping us entertained with games of spinning tops, wooden trains, carved farm animals and other delights of childhood which we treasured. All toys were shared except for the rag doll Rosa carried with her at all times, the doll I hated, for its laughing face seemed at odds with the world we lived in at times. I envied the closeness of the twins, envied the fact they communicated with no more than a look, a touch, that they shared common thoughts, spoke at the same time, stopped at the same time, even sat across the table from one another would begin to eat the same thing at the same time. David was amused, from his oh so superior position as head of the house, when our parents were at work: I just felt insignificant and lost at times, being the last one, the baby of the family.

Summer days, playing with friends in their gardens, drinking home-made lemonade, eating fine cakes and Jewish food from the local baker and kosher shop. Sound of Hebrew as natural to me as German, hearing it from the parents of friends, from their friends who came calling with their children, one huge happy friendly family, all trying to make a living in a hard time when work was scarce and we Jews were not universally liked. Still they laughed and dreamed and spoke of the good days ahead. I spent most of my childhood, the early years when I did not understand, waiting for these good days to come, wondering what treats they would bring poor Daniel, the baby of the family, the one who had the cast-off clothes and the toys the older ones no longer wanted. I remember the laughter, the closeness, the

76

word 'dream' often mentioned, and 'the good days to come'. Ah, we are a people who have lived on dreams all our history.

We still do.

Autumn days, leaves changing, falling, coolness and chill mornings, sunshine, my own coat with a curly fur collar to snuggle into against the coldness, everyone muffled up against the cold to come. One sharp morning and out came the winter coats, scarves, gloves and boots. Mother would insist on our wearing our winter clothes even when it was not really so very cold, not yet. Just that lovely Autumn chill.

Such a performance to go out! All four children had to be dressed in winter coats, hats with flaps for the ears, gloves, scarves, boots. Rosa always wanted to look good, was always in front of the mirror, admiring the dark curls and dark eyes which everyone said were her special features. Poor Rosa, no one had the heart to tell her she would never turn heads, would never win any competitions, would never attract whistles down the road. We knew it, we all knew it, from a very early age, for poor Rosa was Solomon's twin and looked just like him. Square face, thick neck, thick hair, typical Jewish nose, very unfeminine. But I have to say here and now I loved Rosa more than either David or Solomon, for Rosa was full of heart, full of giving, full of energies of life which spilled over to all around her. I don't believe she saw herself then as anything but pretty, never thought of herself as anything other than feminine and who were we to disillusion her? Oh my dear sister, it has been good to be reunited with you! You know what I speak is the truth, you have never been truly blind to your own shortcomings, but that is only the face you present to the world. Inside you were always the most wonderful of people.

Rosa was, as I said, like Solomon and was ever anyone more aptly named! Always solemn, always serious, everything judged and thought about from the first. Give Solomon a toy and he would consider it from every angle, study the lines, the shape, the movement of it, set it down and stare at it as if waiting for it to perform on its own. A strange boy, with serious, strangely logical thoughts. Not for Solomon the joys of fairy tales and myths and legends, he was ever with his head in books which told of facts: science, geography, history - I once asked him if history was all fact, were not the historians writing what they considered to be history? This was when we were much older and able to have such conversations. It was at some family gathering or other and he was again with a book under his arm, some hefty tome of philosophy. He looked at me as if I had said I had met the Messiah. Then logic took over and he shook his head.

"If I can't believe in the written word of these men, there is no point in my reading any written words ever again."

Oh my brother, my dear beloved brother, I am glad you did not live to see what men who had written history made of the new history being written - using the blood of the Jews, the Poles, the unfortunates, to do it.

The David of the Bible went out to slay a giant with no more than a stone and a sling. My brother David was well named, for many times did he try to take on giants, with or without a sling, and sometimes won and sometimes lost. He looked like a Jew, for we as a race have interbred to some degree and ended up with a sort of stereotype, all the women are small, round and fat with prominent noses and dark hair and all the men have hook noses, long beards and dark hair. David, of course, did not have a beard at that age - but to fit the stereotype he grew one as a teenager, much to Mother's mixed feelings, for he looked so much like Grandfather Moishe it was not true. He also had Grandfather Moishe's temper and could not stand back when the taunts of 'kike' and 'Jewboy' were thrown at him at school or outside the gates, where no teacher bothered to intervene for then it was nothing to do with them. Not that they intervened much at school either, we can see, looking back, how the 'standing back and letting the Jews take it' was taking part of their minds and souls already.

I diverted: talking of my dear sister and then my brothers, diverted from other memories which was where we started.

Winter. The cold of Potsdam in winter. Biting cold that penetrated every layer of clothing to bite the bones and nip the skin and chill the blood as it raced frantically around the body in an effort to warm it. Oh the snows of winter in Potsdam, huge mountains of it, everything blanketed and the men with shovels clearing the roads for people to walk, struggle, fight their way through the freezing clinging mass of flakes to shop, to visit, to go to work.

And the visiting was so important at that time! Hanukah approaching, time for celebration, for family togetherness and the joy I remember, the light-heartedness I remember, the happiness of being part of such a big loving family.

But when the festival was over, the cold seemed to grind us down, pulling at our hearts and our souls, the relentless cold bitter grey skies, the cold bitter teethed wind, the cold bitter fingers that crept under the many layers of clothes and caught at the skin to chill and to bite and to say, 'you will never escape!'

There were many deaths in the winter in Potsdam: many an old person found frozen beside a meagre fire, for food was expensive and scarce, companionship hard to find for who would venture out on such a bitter night to talk to someone who was not family?

Yet Spring, with all its glory, was coming, even if the long lonely days dragged out in coldness denied that fact at times. Mother and Father would go to work,

79

struggling through the snow, the cold and the rain to earn the money to keep us. David, Rosa and Solomon would go to school and I would be left to be cared for by one or other of the countless aunts, uncles, cousins, even neighbours if no one else was around to take care of little Daniel.

That is why I said the winter days were lonely.

There is a cadence, a rhythm to the days of the week, the weeks of the month, the months of the year which in turn are regulated by the seasons. There is a cadence in the lilting sounds of Yiddish and even of guttural German, a rhythm caused by the higher female voices and the lower gruff male voices, countermanding one another, counter mingling with one another to produce a sound I will never ever forget. Any more than I can forget the smell of kosher cooking, or the hot lemon tea in glasses with silver handles, or the thick milk drinks given to us children to make us strong and healthy to withstand the Potsdam winters.

Everything comes to an end, even the terrible winter days finally gave way under the influence of Spring: slowly the grass reappeared from its long hibernation, trees you would have thought dead slowly emerged into life again, each bud and leaf creeping slowly from its shelter as if afraid of what it might see.

And as the leaves emerged, so we emerged from our winter clothes into the lighter ones of the warmer days. Windows were opened again, the sweet smell of nature came surging through the place, driving out the cloying winter smells of warm wool drying, of ash and coal, of bodies long kept too close together. It was only when it all changed did you realise how cloying and close it had all become.

Spring is still my favourite time of year, when everything is new grown and new blown and the life seems to surge through everything and everyone, as if the buildings took on new life, as if the streets were made of rubber, you could bounce along them.

And in the Spring the persecutions began again. In the winter the ones who hated the Jews were locked inside their homes as we were, afraid of the cold, afraid of the slippery streets, afraid of those who lurked in dark alley-ways to pounce on the unaware, those who might have gold to steal. In Spring we were all out again and those who hated us would walk the streets, calling out their vicious names, sometimes chalking their vicious comments on the walls. And I, coming up to being five years old, saw this and did not understand.

Now I do.

By the time I reached five, my brother David had been at school for some years. I envied his ability to read anything he picked up, envied his easy way of handling money, figures, knew facts and data about the world around us, could quote all sorts of things at me from history or geography. I felt insignificant, stupid, useless in some ways. Rosa and Solomon had also had some schooling but were not as advanced as he, who had the brain of quicksilver for facts and figures anyway, always did. Kindly relatives would pat my head, so different from my brothers and sister's, and say 'ah but our Daniel is different, he has a different gift' as if I could not read or write and never would. I knew some words, could spell my name, could write my address, I had the beginnings of letters before I went to school. So I would hide around chairs and jump out on them, take their cups of tea before they could pick them up, hide their books and papers, play tricks to make them laugh. And deep inside knew the moment I got to school I would be a model scholar, I would study hard and learn well and be as good as David any day of the week.

Chapter 8

School was a surprise.

I had thought to be studying all the time, learning the words, the letters, the numbers that would lead me into life. It was all there, of course, but the games, the physical exercise of running and playing, of so many children around me, far more than I ever knew existed, was a shock. We were in huge classrooms, jammed behind desks, sitting with ink wells and steel-nibbed pens, with rough paper which splattered the ink everywhere as we struggled to form the letters the teacher put on the board.

School was a surprise - but a good one. I could see how I could learn, for the class was so large I could lose myself among the other children until the knowledge sunk in, then I could be one whose hand shot up each time with an answer, as I saw others do, saw they got books we didn't get, worked out that they were the ones who had tutors at home or at least parents who could work with them. Not like ours, at work every moment of every day. But for all that, I found out our home had more love than theirs and that is all that matters in the end.

School was slate, smell of chalk, of close proximity bodies, scraping of feet, coughs and sneezes, hectoring voices, squeak of blackboard, stamping running of many children escaping to playgrounds to give themselves a break and let the teachers gather to talk. School was the effort of translating what was on the board to sensible signs on the slate, then on the paper with the ink which splattered everywhere. It was a time of opening up, for my world opened up like a flower in the sun, the knowledge poured in and the well was never full.

School was routine, day after day, getting up and getting ready at the same time, to venture out into the world at the same time and go to the same building. Unlike being cared for by motley relatives, school put an order into my life which I liked.

What I didn't like was being constantly compared with my brothers and sister. 'David is good at maths' would come the sort of condemnation I grew to hate. 'You need to work harder, Daniel.' But Daniel was working to the very limit of his ability, something they did not seem to want to understand. Our parents wanted us to do well, of course they did, but they did not realise or understand or appreciate that every mind is different, that we have talents which are not always shared by others. David had the quicksilver mind. My mind would never be that fast but it was enough, oh it was enough to keep me in the middle of the class, where there is less attention drawn to you from the other children – and that was very important. Be too good at things and you are hated, be too bad at things and you are both pitied and scorned. Be average, on the surface, and all is well, for you fit in. So I drank in the knowledge but never let it be seen that I was capable of more than I did, for that way lay disaster for a Jewish boy in a German school at that time.

There was one piece of knowledge that escaped me for the longest time, only arriving later on in a burst of shrapnel which blew all preconceived ideas out of the window. This may not be the right point in the story to state such a fact but it is an essential part of what I became, so –

I found out that history can and was and is distorted, that what I read in books was not necessarily a true record of what really happened. It was then I asked the critical question of my oh so solemn brother Solomon and had his answer. From then on I kept such thoughts to myself.

More Memories.

Recalling the time Grandfather Luka died. Until that time, my life had been lived in a cocoon of love, of sunlight even on the coldest bitterest Potsdam days, for the love and security which surrounded me cushioned me against the cold light of the Reaper. Oh yes, I knew people froze to death by their heaths in the winter months, but I didn't know them and if I did, they had not edged their way into the cosy world in which I lived. Grandfather Luka was my father's father, a dignified man with a shock of white hair and piercing blue eyes that saw into your very soul. He seemed almost stern on the surface but he was all love, pure love, especially for the grandchildren in the family. He had taken a meal with us on the Thursday, one Mother had cooked with her usual loving care and bright smile. Grandfather and Grandmother had come in their second best clothes, looking as they always did, calm, safe, eternal. Next morning a cousin brought the news that Grandfather Luka had died in his sleep. Grandmother had woken, gone to the other room for a drink of water, come back and realised that her husband had slipped away while she had been gone for that short time.

It was like a huge hole bored in my life.

It was almost unbelievable to me that he could – should – go away and leave me like that, leave me with only one grandfather, that he could go to another place, another time, and leave little Daniel here in this place, in this time. I was just seven years old and unknowing of other worlds, other realms, but being brought up in a family where God was another member, I knew there had to be somewhere for us to go. It was simply not possible to believe that such an important person – to me – could simply be no more. He had to be more, but more somewhere else. No one could tell me where he had gone, no one could interrupt their mourning, or stop the reciting of Kaddish for his soul, to tell me where my grandfather had gone.

Grandmother donned even more black, if that was possible, a veritable night time's worth of black cascading over her. Black crepe hung from bonnets, from sleeves, from coats and even shawls and the cascade flowed over other family members, too. Black ties, black everything.

And Father went by day to the factory of Ivan Ivanovitch where he stitched black cloth and hid his sorrowing among the rolls of darkness which filled the shop.

Mother smiled her way through a day of hats and frills and falderals and let tears drop gently down her face so she could dry them with a small lace edged hankie and have the other ladies in the milliners sympathise with her. How do I know? I went visiting and saw for myself.

My siblings were distraught and refused to play or do anything but sit and stare at the walls. I saw no tears, just oh so sad faces.

I had no place to hide my sorrow. I had to bury it deep inside, go to school with the smile and the laugh and the tricks and the pretence that all was well, what was the death of a grandparent, after all? 'Oh yes,' said the other boys, indifferent, uncaring, almost callous. 'My grandfather died two years ago,' boasted one, 'and we had this huge funeral! Half the street turned out for it!'

More than half the street turned out for Grandfather Luka's internment in the cold unwelcoming ground that rendered itself steep and harsh and which seemed to absorb my grandfather begrudgingly. The rabbi intoned his prayers and I heard nothing but the sound of Grandfather's voice telling me not to worry, not to cry, not to mourn his passing for he had been tired and his body had given up because it was worn out.

I could say nothing of what I heard for fear of ridicule and scorn, for that would have spoiled the precious words that came to me. But after that the smiles and the tricks became real, not just make-believe for the sake of those around me. I knew then what I know now – that there was an after-life; that the dead did not die but lived on, in another dimension, another world.

And in memory I recall that Grandmother did not stay long on this earth without her beloved husband. Before too long, it seemed almost like the next day, so fast did the time go, we were once again standing around an open grave, listening to the same prayers being intoned by the same rabbi. Only the name changed and the fact that no Grandmother stood by her son's side. He was now standing by his wife's side, having lost both parents in a very short space of time.

The dark rolls of material blotted many more tears, I do believe.

But this time I shed few tears. This time, the Reaper did not come to tear a hole in my cocoon, for Grandfather Luka's passing had done that and I knew I would lose more family.

After the sadness of my grandparents, the passing of an aunt or uncle was of little account, although I was aware the happy laughing group that had surrounded me from birth was slowly diminishing, one at a time. Dinner tables were less crowded at the great festivals or just a Sabbath joining together for the meal: the rooms had more space now than they ever did.

And I grew up to be a solitary child, left out of the games of others, not part of my siblings' life for David was big, bold and off out into the world with boys of his own age and the twins had each other. Somehow there never was room for Daniel when the twins were together, or even apart.

86

I wonder now why I was not included in the games of other boys in our street, for there were many there: rough ones, quiet ones, tall ones, very short ones who seemed to have more energy than all the others put together. They played their football, their catch, tag and other games which sent boys spiralling and spinning in all directions, shouting and screaming at one another as they went. But I was not part of any of it, despite being the resident family clown. Maybe I was too different, I was almost going to say too Jewish but that would have been a lie. For my siblings were Jewish to their very bones whereas I was different.

Perhaps in that lies the answer to my own question: was I too different for them, perhaps the blond hair bothered them, or the face that did not have the seemingly traditional racial features. But equally I was not one of them. In my heart I was a German Jew; in my mind I was just Daniel, someone who wanted so much to belong to something, someone. Did that mean I did not feel part of my family? Of course I did, for we were loving and loved one another without reservation. But we were a small, very small, part of the great cosmos and I longed to be part of the wider world, the groups I saw around Potsdam. I wanted to be one of the boys. I stood watching them play, without the nerve to go and say 'hey, to me!' when the football was kicked or be around when they chose teams. Without the nerve for I feared them turning away, their rejection of me. If they did not call to me, surely that meant they did not want me. After all, I was stood there, waiting, available, accessible to a kicked football that would have been swiftly returned and I would have become part of the team. It never happened so the words 'hey, to me!' were always in my head and never in my mouth. And the hurt stayed in my heart and in my eyes that burned with the need to cry but no boy ever cried in front of others unless his nose was broken or his mother had died.

And so I walked, way beyond the clustered houses which made up our quarter of the city, walked and walked and saw things they did not: the birds, the small animals, the pet dogs which escaped and went on adventures of their own, slinking cats and once a dog fox. Saw the changes of the days, how they were never the same, how the clouds made patterns in the sky and the wind caught and played with trees, blooms, washing strung on lines and I knew I could write of these things, if it were not a childish or unmanly thing to want to do. I knew little at that time of the great poets; it was not something our schoolteachers passed on to us boys and I did not realise it would be a great thing to do. It would also have been a release but I knew nothing of that, either. I was no more than a boy, lonely, afraid inside, knowing things were not right in my world but equally not knowing of the great movements, political and otherwise, which were causing the problems. Children rarely see beyond their immediate world, no matter how psychic they might be. Even then I missed my Grandfather Luka with an aching hurt that would not be satisfied. That did not help very much; the walks became very lonely at times, for I was not able to feel his presence or hear his voice as I had done at the funeral. Maybe the loneliness, the fear and the anxiety got between Grandfather and little Daniel's mind at that time.

I got wet at times and learned to love the feel of rain on my face and head. I got cold at times and appreciated the shelter offered by bushes, hedges and houses. I got hot and welcomed the feel of cold water from creeks and springs on my face and hands. And I built a love for nature that has never ever died.

After the walks, I would go home to David, Solomon, Rosa and my loving parents, home to the little flat which had become a sanctuary against the slings and arrows of outrageous people, home to the little truckle bed which was my ultimate sanctuary, where I could revisit everywhere I had just visited in the precious time before sleep captured my weary soul.

So we were a happy family during those years, despite losing family members one by one to the great mystery called Death. Happy in that there was enough food, warm clothes, books and, most of all, strength, to go around. We knew we were barely tolerated. Mother and Father were as aware as us children of the problems outside, in the German world that did not happily live with us Jews. But we could not leave, for where would we go? We had no family anywhere else, no roots anywhere else. Could we just go and move away, leaving Grandfather Luka and dear Grandmother in the ground, lonely and alone without one of us to call by and visit the grave from time to time? And the other members who became involved in the great mystery called Death; we could not leave them, either. Our roots were in Potsdam, and in particular, in this little corner of Potsdam where we worked, schooled, played and had our leisure time, such as it was.

So we endured the silences at times, the taunts of other children, the disapproving looks of officialdom in all its many faces, and went on living our lives, ones surrounded by the traditions of our race and the comforting presence of family.

In that way the years melted away, people grew older without our realising it at the time, grey sprinkled the black and brown, hunched over replaced upright and outside, in the big world, the first rumblings of real problems began to make themselves felt.

And I grew from a shy, hesitant, lonely boy to a self-contained, shy, self-conscious young man. Very young, still not what is now called a teenager, but at that time you passed into adulthood a lot earlier, for a living had to be earned and life was not easy. Father still worked for the Russian tailor, Mother still wrought pretty hats for the milliner but the money was not going up in line with the cost of living and many a time David, Solomon, Rosa and myself went scouring for branches, cones, bits of scrap wood and paper, anything that would burn, so that we could keep warm during the long Potsdam winters.

David had a job, working for a local butcher, delivering the meat to customers. He carried it in a big basket he balanced on his head. Often he would return, talking of the big houses he had visited, how much money the people had, the warmth which came out of the door when they opened it to the young man who knocked, of the servants he saw and the good life some people had. I tried to tell him they probably had less love in their homes than we did, but it did not make any difference. There came a burning desire in my beloved brother to have money such as they did and live in homes like that.

"You will have to study and become a lawyer or doctor," Father said, overhearing this conversation one night. And David did just that. He became a student, working his way through many books of heavy law: civil and criminal, until the day came he got a job with a lawyer, who was astonished at how much he already knew.

Solomon had no such plans for life. He was bound to be a professor of history and so it turned out, for he studied history all day and every day, for pleasure and for school, for leisure and for learning. He could not get enough of the past but my dear brother could not see what was happening around him in the present.

And Rosa. The family had such plans for their only girl, such high plans of her making the perfect marriage, of the white dress she would wear and the great reception we would have. All this long before Rosa entered puberty! But girls at that time were only expected to become good wives, not to become anything more than that.

But Rosa – my very dear sister – went out to visit a friend one night. Not far, two or three streets away from ours in Potsdam, a warm Spring night when the hint of blossom touched the air, when stars sparkled in the blueness before it became truly dark. A night for romance and for lovers.

But a night which also held a darker side. As she returned home, long before the hour when doors were locked against intruders, long before many would consider turning to their beds, Rosa was attacked by a group of Jew hating Germans and raped and beaten and left for dead.

It was Mother who found her, Mother on the way back from a mercy mission to a neighbour all but fell over her daughter lying on the pavement, bleeding, battered and incoherent. She managed to half carry – half walk her home and put her to bed, bathed her wounds, attended to her physical state as best she could while knowing only time would heal the mental state.

We did not inform the police. The family closed ranks to protect Rosa; cousins found themselves acting as detectives and seeking out the perpetrators for themselves. One by one they were 'dealt with' in back streets of Potsdam or in an alleyway late at night. The family were revenged without bringing the authorities in, people who would have made sympathetic noises, pretended to make notes and who would have gone away and ignored it. No, it was better our way.

David was furious. He stormed and shouted, and seemed almost ready to go out and commit murder. It took all our doing to calm him, for he could not be seen to be involved in the retribution we were planning. He understood, but it did not calm him.

Rosa lay in bed many a long week. She stared at the walls as if not seeing them, she stared at us as if we were strangers. Only Mother could get near her, could reach inside the pain and hurt, the shock and sheer horror of it, to comfort her beloved daughter. Not even Solomon could reach his twin, it was as if she had shut herself down from all human contact.

After about three months of being housebound she managed to get the strength to walk outside in the sunshine. She began to talk again, to look to some kind of future, to go to school once more and pick up the studies she had so abruptly dropped. My beloved sister would have made a fine nurse or worker with animals, she had compassion and healing in her hands and her heart. It was stolen from her in one brutal act of lust and hatred. But we thought it was going all right, we thought we were getting there, the family relaxed, breathed a sigh of relief, poor Father lost his haunted look.

But just as we thought everything really was going along just fine, the doctor confirmed what Mother had suspected – Rosa was pregnant.

It was a burden not to be borne. Mother collapsed and was in bed for a week, with her job hanging in the balance for the ladies sought her fine hands with the millinery and the ribbons. She gave some excuse about over work and bereavement catching up on her, for no one wanted to tell the truth. Poor Father's haunted look came back – and stayed. David was all set to go on a killing spree and had to be forcibly restrained by uncles who knew only too well what such a dire act would bring to the family. And my beloved brother walked around as if half his life had been taken from him.

In some ways it had, for none can divine the closeness of twins if you were not one yourself. I always felt excluded from the two of them, reached Solomon only on a family level, not on a deeply emotional level. It was as if the two of them had taken a chunk of love, carved it into two and consumed half each, with none left over for anyone else.

But Rosa's terrible night of terror and hatred had poisoned her chunk of love. Her body turned on her, she lost all power to eat, to drink; she became a skeleton, her beautiful dark eyes looking out from a soul gone to acid.

Three months after the diagnosis the baby left Rosa's body in a rush of blood in the middle of a Sunday dinner and three hours after that Rosa's spirit departed the body completely and my sister was at last released from her torment.

If Grandfather Luka's passing had torn a hole in my young life, Rosa's all but destroyed it. For three long months we had lived with the prospect of a child that was unwanted and unprepared for but which would have been loved as something our Rosa had given life to. We had discussed, as a family, where the baby would sleep, what we would do to accommodate the new arrival, how we would manage. Family had come with suggestions and small gifts: Rosa had begun to compile a baby chest of items, all gratefully received. But the haunted look never left her eyes and her voice never rose above a whisper – when she did speak. Mostly she walked around our home like a rootless ghost, walking here and there as if her body refused to allow her to rest, as if by walking all day, pacing the floor endlessly, she could work out of her system all that was hurting her so much. Food appeared to poison her, she would stare at it as though it was alien to her and pick at the edges of the meal prepared with such love. She grew thinner, became gaunt, became nothing more than eyes in a skull.

Solomon would sit opposite her at the table, as he had always done, willing her with his deep eyes to eat, eat Rosa, eat! Not a word passed between them but we all read the message as clearly as if it had been shouted aloud from the rooftops. But Rosa appeared not to hear, not to be able to comprehend that she needed the food to help balance the acid that tore at her heart and her mind and eventually her soul.

No one outside, apart from the doctor, knew of the baby, for not a curve or a scrap of fat showed on her painfully thin body to reveal the presence of a life.

Did her own hatreds kill the child, expel it from her body? Or was the child itself unwilling to come to the earth, to be born into a life that would have been – to put it simply – difficult? How could a child of a rape survive in our society, where the Jews were barely tolerated, where the Germans looked down on us, where such a mixture would have belonged to neither side?

I could almost sense the relief – it was almost palpable around the table – as Rosa clutched her abdomen and the blood gushed out of her onto the worn carpet. Mother ran for towels, Father sat and looked helpless in the face of such an overwhelming female problem. Solomon sat as if turned to stone and I wanted to cry.

"Run for the doctor, Daniel," Mother instructed as she picked up her almost lifeless daughter and carried her to the bedroom. I saw Father's slight nod as I left the table, the food half eaten and gone cold in the shock of what was happening.

I ran through pouring rain, sliding on worn smooth pavements, dodging people under their umbrellas, seeing their surprise at the hatless coatless boy running as if the Devil himself were chasing along the Potsdam streets.

The doctor's house was white, tall, clean and highly polished. But no one came to the highly polished door to respond to the ringing of the polished brass bell. I rang with all the desperation that had built in me from the moment the first event had happened, but no one came.

I ran home, soaked with rain and tears, (for in the rain no one knows you are crying, do they?) to break the news that the doctor was not there.

"It will be too late anyway," Mother said, the words coming from a bone white face. "There will be little he could do for my Rosa."

I grabbed a towel to dry my head and went to change my clothes. When I went back to the table, Father and Solomon were still sat as they had been when I had left what felt like an hour earlier. But when I touched my dinner, it was still warm. So short a time to be gone, to go through every emotion a child can go through and still come out the other side.

Then I realised Father was crying openly and I found there were still emotions I had not touched, for to see a man cry is enough to tear the heart from any son.

Solomon never cried. Not then, not later when the frail body was carried out, not when the prayers for the dead were chanted, not when Rosa went to her resting place, nor in the long years following. It was as if Rosa had taken the tears with her passing. No matter what happened, Solomon never cried. He went even quieter than before and buried himself in his books, studying, studying, studying to be the best professor of History Potsdam had ever had.

My sister was fifteen years old when she passed. Solomon was fifteen years old, too young to be so solemn and serious about life. I was still young but growing fast.

The year was 1914.

Chapter 9

War Years.

I think we all knew war was coming before it got there, even us kids who didn't bother over much with politics and government and things like that. But there was an air of expectancy, of apprehension, of danger, much shaking of heads and muttering over thick glasses of tea and dark beers when the family called round.

At first I blamed the feeling on Rosa's death, for that hung like a thick pall of heavy black smoke over our little home. No one laughed, no one smiled, no one even said it was a bright sunny day, no one spoke unless they had to.

Mother had gone back to work in the milliners, suffering the condolences and fussing of Frau Heinemann and the customers, busy fingers creating busy hats and head coverings for German ladies and Jewish ladies who would not be seen out without a head covering of some kind. I think they would have felt naked had they gone out with nothing on their heads, much as I would had I gone to school without my skull-cap. All these things have fancy Jewish names, you know that, there is no need for me to spell them out for you all. And if I used the fancy names you would not know to what I refer, so let it be said in plain English for all to understand!

Again I divert. But the story is hard in the telling and at times I divert to ease my mind as well as the mind of the channel.

Father had gone back to work but the bales of dark cloth had gone, replaced by the horrid material used for German Army uniforms. Such was the demand for new uniforms for the new army that every tailor in Germany had been issued with instructions to provide them.

Father was working on uniforms for the officers, the smart jackets and trousers. Where then would his tears fall when memories walked too hard? But we were glad they were both working for at least we could buy what was needed to eat, be dressed, be warm and safe in all the weather. And the gentlemen who went to be measured for new dark suits had to wait their turn: the supreme German Army came first.

In the streets, the games of football, tag and other boys' pastimes were discarded for playing at war. Solemnly they marched up and down, carrying toy rifles or bits of wood carved to look like rifles, with the bigger ones shouting orders to the smaller ones. Shouting 'bang!' at each other, the war games went on, while the real war got under way.

Oh how the neighbours lined the streets, cheering and shouting as their sons marched away to fight in a war no one appeared to understand! Or if they did, no one explained it to Daniel, or anyone around him. "The Kaiser" was all I heard and all I understood. And I developed a fierce and unreasoning hatred for this faceless person, for he hid behind his advisers and councillors, behind the military men who wanted to play at soldiers and wanted real people to play it with, not toy soldiers on a mocked up battlefield. I hated him for he was taking away my idols at that time, older boys, almost men, I looked up to even though they never noticed me. The swaggering, confident young men who hung around the drinking clubs and – hush – gambling dens, the ones who had the pretty women hanging on their arms, with cigarettes hanging from their lips and charm pouring from their eyes. These were the men who marched off to war and who came back – sometimes – with haunted eyes, with wooden crutches and wooden limbs or chairs with wheels.

But that was later, much later, when the war began to get going, when we realised it was not a five minute wonder after all, but a long term serious battle against the rest of the world.

Or so it seemed from our corner of Potsdam, anyway.

I know much now of the politics of what is universally known as the First World War. I know now why politicians could not agree and would not agree and how Germany sought to extend its boundaries and take over more territory, I know these things now, having learned much since coming here, to the Higher Realms.

But at the time it started, I was twelve years old, going on thirteen, war had just broken out and the talk was of victory, of glory and of the everlasting greatness of Germany.

I had no reason to disbelieve anything I heard, for no one told me anything different. For that reason, as this is the story of my life, I can only say how I saw the First World War, from a boy's perspective, small though it might be.

David went to war.

He came home in uniform and Mother burst into tears and ran and hid in the bedroom. We could hear her sobbing from outside the door and none of us had the strength or the will to go in and see her to comfort her. I was embarrassed and stood around, wanting to touch, wanting to be touched but never quite managing to let anyone know that was what I wanted.

David went to war.

How simple that sentence but how it ripped the family apart all over again! Cousins had gone but somehow that had not touched us, close family that we were, too.

He marched away with the others one fine sunny morning, with our neighbours lining the streets to cheer them on. Proud they walked, proud and sure, heads up, shoulders back, uniforms immaculate under the sun. I did not cheer but I was proud, so proud my heart almost burst from my chest.

Solomon stood alongside me and he did not cheer either.

One old lady who lived not too far from us smiled at us both. "You boys be grateful you're not old enough to go and fight," she said in an old person's voice, all wavery and quavery. "So many won't be coming back." And that was the moment when the true idiocy of war struck home to me. David, my beloved brother, might not be coming back. In that moment I understood Mother's tears and wished I had gone to her to comfort and hold her as she had held me so many, many times in the past.

Regrets. I've had too many to reckon.

So we were left. We were four now, with uncles, aunts and the remaining very ancient grandparents all living close by. Four felt empty after six. Four was not even half of six yet the rooms felt abandoned, lonely, soulless at times.

Grandparents died, uncles died, Mother and Father worked on and no word came to us from the Front to tell us if David was still alive or had died under the guns of the enemy.

For all of you reading this in the countries who fought the Germans, forgive me. Remember, please, I was only a boy in a small town in Germany, who knew nothing of the big world, who knew only what teachers and other adults told me. You too probably went through the war thinking of Germans as 'the enemy.' And we were, to you, as you were to us. Those who go to war must accept the other side is 'the enemy' until the government, the officials, the dictator, whoever is in control, tells you otherwise. Unless you live in a place where the enmities go so deep it is impossible to ignore, like Yugoslavia and Czechoslovakia, to give them their old names. Then there is no forgiveness and no ending of hostility.

I divert, yet again, as I do when something so hurtful comes around I have to divert, for my sake and for the sake of my channel. Again, I ask forgiveness of my reader.

It was a time of good fortune for me. Old enough to run errands, to work part time in the bakery, running here and there with bread when I was not at school – and at that time I was not at school much, for many teachers were fighting on the Front Line against the foreigners. Errands and the few hours of work brought money in which I gave to Mother for the family, for food prices had risen dramatically, either through genuine shortages or enterprising suppliers making a lot of money from those of us still at home.

Father had plenty of work, making uniforms and in between, making the dark suits for the important Burghers of our town, for they needed their smart suits as much as the Army needed smart uniforms. Mother did not have as much work but enough to keep her busy and the chit-chat in the shop helped pass the days, ease the hurt, for I know she missed Rosa and David dreadfully.

I left school at 14, not wanting any more lessons, any more dull classes, any more lectures on the great German race. The persecutions steadily worsened: we were called so many names I cannot begin to recite them now for fear of causing much anger and rage not only in my reader but in myself. It was not a good time. It was as if the Germans, the pure bred Germans, as they saw themselves, had developed a hatred of everything which was 'foreign' and that included Jews, Poles, Russians, Czechs and anyone else foolish enough to have been born in their country but with immigrant background or lineage. There were attacks aplenty on anyone who walked the streets. It became a nightmare just existing.

Then Ivan Ivanovitch was killed. Outside his little tailor's shop, locking the doors one night, they jumped him and hacked him to death with axes and knives, spray painting 'Russian pig' on the door afterwards.

We heard nothing but those who did said they could not go to his aid for fear of being killed themselves, for the drunken rowdy youths who committed the murder were in no fit state to be reasoned with. And the police would have been too long in coming to save him,

Father went to the funeral, attended by only two others. He said it was a sad, lonely affair. He had died wifeless, childless and virtually friendless, but he had worked in Potsdam for many years, outfitting the men and uniforming the Army. Thus are the people rewarded who labour for others!

For a week the shop remained tight shut, then Father was summoned to a meeting. The lawyers had taken over by then and were ready to do business.

Father talked of it later but it did not need much imagination to picture the dark rolls of cloth absorbing the high legal talk, the fancy words, the facts and figures. The old Russian had left instructions that the business was to be sold to any worker who could raise the money to buy it.

There were three Jews at the meeting and a German lawyer. Father said how the lawyer looked down his patrician nose at the Jews, at their skullcaps and shawls, at their curls and austere faces and expected a denial that any would take on the shop. But he was shocked to his roots by Father standing up and declaring that he had money and, if it was sufficient, he would take on the business and work with his fellow Jews in a collective way to keep the shop open and the people of Potsdam garbed if they so wanted.

We had money for Mother had hoarded everything I had contributed, all that David had given her before his departure to the Front, and all that she could save from the money we all had to live on.

It was enough.

We had a business.

We were a step up in the social standing of the town of Potsdam.

And no one – but no one – acknowledged it.

It didn't matter one iota, for we knew what we were, they knew what we were. It showed in the reaction when Father went to work in the morning, as he unlocked the door of his own business, for the attitude of those who came in, those who saw him, was more deferential, not much but enough to acknowledge the difference without any one person coming right out and saying it. He was never invited to sit on any committees dealing with the commerce of Potsdam, he was silently excluded from that, but as I said, it didn't matter one iota. The business continued to be known as The Russian Tailor's and the work turned out was the same as before.

The difference was a lighter atmosphere without the shouting, brooding, slave driving Russian there and the consultation between all three of them, Father and his two associates, on how the work was divided up, who would cut, who would stitch, who would deliver, if they needed someone else and when and who and how things were to be carried out made it work. Nothing was done without consultation and the orders multiplied and the workers grew one by one. Father took on the shop next door and made it part of the tailoring business.

And still the good burghers of Potsdam refused to acknowledge the new businessman in their midst.

So life continued until the end of the Great War, the one we were supposed to win and didn't, the one which brought down the wrath of the Gods, or so it seemed, on German heads as they bowed in defeat.

102

And what happens when proud people have to acknowledge defeat? They look for scapegoats. So many of us in their midst became the target for their injured wounded pride! All the Turkish workers, the immigrants from all the other countries, the roaming people, the poor, the Jews, the Christians from the different sects, I could go on but you know the sad litany of those who were vilified and pilloried by the proud Germans.

And so the war dragged to its terrible end and David came home.

No. Someone called David came home but it was not my brother, not the bright eyed proud fierce fighter of all who came before him who came home.

The David who came home was a shambling broken shell of a man, walking with a severe limp from a shell wound to the thigh, leaning on a stick like an old man. Thin he was, thin to emaciation so that we were afraid to touch or hug for fear of breaking a bone in his fragile looking body.

But it was not the physical condition which shocked us all but the blank staring look from the soul behind the eyes.

David, my dear daring darling brother, had seen too much and felt too much and heard too much and been shocked by too many deaths and so much suffering around him that he could and would never be the same again.

It took us some time to realise just how bad it was.

For a long time, life returned to a semblance of normality, as far as it can do with a shell-shocked war-shocked person sat staring blindly at the wall for hours on end. Mostly we tiptoed around him and let him get on with it, but Mother suddenly took it into her head to cajole him out of it, to treat him like the small boy he had once been. She tried to entice him into going for walks through the prettier parts of Potsdam, or visit neighbours with her or look in at the shop when Father was working late. She even suggested he return to his old job with the lawyer and received such a fierce look of hatred and despair that she ran crying from the room and did not appear again for hours.

For a long time, we all went to work and made out life was normal. Solomon found work in a library, where he could read his history between dealing with customers; I was now working with Father in the shop, learning the art of tailoring and helping out as best I could, especially with deliveries. Mother was still at the milliners, although I was aware of the greying hair and the haggard lines in her face as her troubled mind continued to worry at the problems surrounding her family.

And we had no choice but to leave David at home with his thoughts.

There seemed nothing he could do – he could have taken on the deliveries from the shop but that would have been demeaning him even further, the thought that after he fought in a war, all he was fit for was deliveries, so I carried on doing those and carried on wondering how long we could leave him alone before the explosion happened.

The situation lasted a year.

I know it was a year because it was that fact which prompted the row.

Mother was still trying to coax David to go out and do some work or visit people, to connect with real life again.

"After all," she said, "it has been a year since you came home and you have done nothing during that time."

She meant no harm, I am sure of that: it was just a comment any of us would have made had we been the ones discussing it with this wild eyed stranger who was once a loving son and brother.

"Done nothing!" he screamed at her and she backed out of the door, away from the wildness we all saw in his face, perhaps afraid of his violence. "Done nothing! I fought in a war and came home again – which is more than the other poor devils did! Done nothing!" and every word took him a step closer to Mother and she took a step back. And another and yet another and they were out in the hall and Mother was still backing away and he was still advancing, shouting wildly and seemingly in a blind rage and before we knew what was happening she had fallen down the stairs and broken her neck.

We did not need to go and look to know she was dead; no one could lie with their head at that angle and still be breathing. But we went anyway, Father and I, while David stood staring with the saddest eyes I have ever seen in my life, and "Done nothing" was replaced with "I didn't mean it". We knew that anyway. It was an accident waiting to happen, to use a modern expression.

Our house was again filled with mourning keening praying relatives and a rabbi trying to calm it all down and offer his prayers for the dead but I, for one, no longer wanted to listen. What sort of God allowed my sister to die, my brother to come home so changed and my mother to have such a tragic accident? I could accept the old ones sliding into death, for their time had come and their bodies were old and weary but my sister was young and should have been full of life and Mother, although wearied by her worries and work, still had years ahead of her.

My readers will know I now know different, that these things are planned and known before we leave the Realms, our time and way of passing set out for us before we leave for the earth plane but then I was a young man with no knowledge of such things and could only shake my fist and rant and rave at the heartless faceless God who had destroyed my family.

105

For a long time I refused to speak to anyone who had any religious leanings. The rabbi got very annoyed with me, told me I was being foolish and should grow up. He should worry: had he lost a sister, a brother and a mother before he became a real man? I was growing up, bitter and hurt and angry at the world.

David withdrew into himself, became a living shell, not eating, not speaking, just sitting in a chair, staring at the wall. All that fine mind rotting away inside a growing cloud of guilt and anger and bitterness. Or that is how I saw it, anyway. As he never spoke, I had to guess and try to understand myself.

Father was completely lost, almost unable to function. Even his beloved tailoring held no joys any more. There was not enough dark material in the world to hide the tears this time.

Solomon carried on with his reading, losing himself in worlds long past, trying to learn from them to make sense of the present and indeed of the future, for the portents were not good.

For a new Germany was rising from the ashes of the old and it boded nothing but evil for those of us who, as before, did not fit in the frame.

There was conflict within me for the longest time. I fought my beliefs, the whole upbringing I had gone through, fought the influences that the synagogue placed on us all, fought my family who tried to say I should accept and be glad the suffering was done. Be glad! I had lost my mother, the one person who illuminated my life and they wanted me to be glad! I would rather it had been me who had been pushed down the stairs than my beloved mother!

I tried to take her place. I shopped and cooked, cleaned and washed and did everything she used to do. In between I spent hours at the tailors, back breaking and eyes straining, fingers stabbed with the needle a hundred times a day until they coarsened up enough to withstand the needle point to some degree. For there were still uniforms to sew, even if they did now want an odd symbol attached to the sleeve.

"Only an old Sun symbol," said one wise uncle, his beard nodding as his head followed. "They are reverting to the old ways." But Uncle was wrong; it was not only an old Sun symbol, for it had been perverted to a new meaning. 'They' were not reverting to old ways but following what they had always done: persecuted the innocent, the different, the helpless and the religious among them. Persecuting all who were not 'pure' as if they themselves were the purest race on the earth. There was conflict outside, in the government, in the streets, in the drinking houses and in the synagogues. Everyone had a different point of view of where it would go and what it would mean for the Jews of Potsdam.

In the house there was no conflict, for no one dared speak of it for fear of what it would do, what it would provoke in David. He had fought in a war and come home a broken man and here we were, sliding to it yet again, as if no lessons had been learned, as if no one had taken a single moment to consider that history was rewriting itself and it was not for the good of Germany.

For a time all was relatively quiet; we worked and we suffered and we grieved. I cooked and everyone ate everything I prepared without a word of complaint, so it could not have been that bad. I learned to shop sensibly, to make the money go as far as possible, storing what I could against the day when money would be needed, for the rumblings were reaching our closed off minds by then and we knew we might have to run and hide before too long.

Father mourned his lost wife but also his lost son, for David was no more than a shell now, no words passed his lips. He ate, he drank, he slept, he washed himself and dressed himself but no more. His son had, to all intents and purposes, died along with his beloved wife.

How sad it is for a firstborn to fail his family in this way! For such high hopes were had for David, especially when he began work with the lawyer and read the law books and became knowledgeable.

And how proud Father was when David came home wearing his uniform and marched away to war with the others. It is true that families never believe that tragedy will strike their son, their heart of hearts, their dreams, in that way. But it is also true that our family seemed to suffer more than most, for here was one tragedy after another.

We spoke – "Thank you, Daniel."

"Have you had enough to eat, Father?"

"Solomon, are you able to deliver a parcel for us tomorrow on your way to the library?"

"Are there clean clothes for the morning for everyone or should I wash?"

Such trivial things which made up the bricks and mortar of our lives, the courtesies, the considerations of one another as living beings who had no hearts any more, kept us going, day after day. And day after day the pain grew a fraction less until the time came when I could look outside my world and be horrified by what I saw.

For the slogans had proliferated; shop windows were being regularly broken; Jews were being attacked in the streets at night.

Fear was returning to the lives of those of us who were of the 'other faith' in this fair land we called home.

Aunts and Uncles would sit around in our tiny flat, commiserating with Father on his many troubles; the Rabbi would call occasionally to find out why we had not gone to the synagogue (none of us could bear to go any more, not even Solomon and he was the most devout of us all up to that time) but no one had a solution to our problems.   And it was true that at that time, we were all looking out for ourselves as much as we could, for the attacks were increasing and the signs were Not Good, no matter which way you read the political climate.   And we would, quietly, discuss what was going on outside.

For Germany was slowly sliding towards another conflict.   How it happened is a tale well known outside the pages of this book, so I will not bore my reader with reciting it all over again.   At least, I will not relate the political side of it all.   We only knew that a madman was making a name for himself and others were following. But we, mourning still, were in no frame of mind to try and work out what he wanted and how it would affect us.   But affect us it did!

Nazis were openly walking the streets of Potsdam, usually in groups, usually drunk, invariably looking for trouble.   Should they spy anyone wearing the shawl, skull cap or even worse, the headband of the truly devout, or the long side curls and tall hat and dark coat, they would be pounced upon with great glee by the persecutors and kicked and punched until they were unconscious, when the Nazis would stride away, making their strange salutes and shouting their strange shouts, leaving their victim for dead in the gutter.

And deaths there were.   Oh, hushed up for the most part, for who wanted to go and make trouble with the authorities when you were clearly a Jew and the authorities were clearly German without a trace of Jewish blood in them and you had no way of knowing whether they leaned toward the Nazis or not, or whether it was politic to do so even if they did not really believe in what was going down there.

It started with the young men at first, for they were often the ones found out on the streets at night.   Young virile men with a life before them, crippled, tortured in mind, rendered useless for anything but being a dependent on their family.

Then it became the older men, those who left the synagogue and meeting houses just before the clubs really got going for the night, trying hard to avoid trouble. They became the targets as much as the young men, for by then the hatred was such that anyone was a target.

We knew, without anyone casting stones or reading the cards, that that the women would be next.

Young girls, raped, abused: tortured, two or three were even killed by gang rapes.

Older women attacked in the street, their skirts thrown up, their most private parts displayed to passers-by. The more comely among them were raped.

Very old women suffered abuse which was heaped on them. That made them afraid to leave their homes.

I have said before in this book and will no doubt say it again – those who believe the problems of the Jews began with the Second World War, think again. We were persecuted from time immemorial and will always be persecuted, for there is an inbuilt racial quality to us that the rest of the world appears to despise for some reason.

Not everyone, I hasten to add! For among my friends then – and now – there are people who are tolerant, who bear no inner or outer thoughts of resentment against what we were and are.

And slowly we realised that our lives were closing in, that orders were fewer, that I had fewer deliveries to do and Solomon had little to do at the library. Father wore his habitual expression of sadness: whether for the loss of Mother or loss of business or loss of a son I did not know – and, to my shame, never did ask. Oh Father, did I fail you as a son as well? I tried, but know that I was not David, never would be David, never would be someone you would be so proud of. I was the worker, the clown, the run around, the chief cook and bottle washer, to quote a British expression. I was not David.

The observant among you will realise I have not mentioned women at all, though we were virile young men on the verge of adulthood. And you are asking yourself, was this Daniel gay, was Solomon so lost in his books that no female would look in his direction?

My answer is – no, I was not gay. Nor was Solomon so lost in his books, but we were so bowed down with sorrow and mourning that we did not feel, any of us, that we could let another woman into our lives. Mother was our sunshine and that had been blotted out. It could not return.

Certainly it could not return while fear rode on the back of sorrow to cause us even more sadness than we already had to cope with! Imagine if either of us had begun a relationship with someone and that someone was attacked and raped in the street or some alleyway where no help would be given, how could we live with ourselves and that person in the future? For it would have brought such shame on the family that it would not have been able to be borne. As it did with Rosa, our dear sister.

Imagine if we took the love of someone into our uncertain future, it would have made that future even more difficult to perceive and anticipate. So, yes, we were virile young men on the verge of adulthood but we were, and remained, virgins – as far as I know. I certainly was and I believe to this day Solomon was, too.

My dear brother was never the same after Rosa died. I was not a twin and cannot begin to know how it feels to have that half of you torn away, thrown into the ground, seemingly lost forever. He must have felt incomplete, I know for the longest time he was inconsolable. Our later tragedies only compounded his sadness and aided and abetted his withdrawal into the books and studies which filled his waking – and for all I know – sleeping hours.

By common unspoken consent, none of us talked of Mother or the war around David, nor did we mention the increase in the young thugs out on the streets, for we had no way of knowing what it would do to the troubled mind which lived in the shattered shell that was my older brother.   Slowly he shrank into himself, became a wrinkled old man so many years before his time, refusing food, refusing even the touch of another human being. Should an aunt call round and try to hug him, he would shrug her away without speaking. I saw the hurt on the faces of those who loved him and felt for them, but also felt bitterness, resentment and anger that they could go home, they could perhaps forget the hurt, whilst we who lived there had to go on living there with the constant reminder of what we had and what we had lost.

It all changed very quickly. I came home one day to start preparing dinner and found David standing at the window, staring out. He had not looked outside since Mother had fallen, it seemed a strange thing for him to do. He stared at me when I came in, as if he didn't recognise me.

"Who – who..." He pointed into the street where a gang of Nazi youths were shouting at passers-by and throwing stones.

"Nazis." I was too shocked by the fact he was standing up, looking out of the window, speaking even, to give him a full answer. But what I had said was enough: he knew, doubtless from sitting in his habitual place by the fire and listening to us and our visitors talking from time to time, what the Nazis meant.

Trouble.

More trouble for Germany, probably with the rest of the world once again.

He said no more, he moved no more from his seat that afternoon and evening. I don't think he went to bed that night. Father, Solomon and I left him sat by the fireside, staring into the flames, thinking who knew what thoughts.

In the morning Father found him dead.

It was as though he had switched himself off in some way, for the Doctor said his heart had simply stopped. No one was to blame, he said, signing the certificate; it was the way of veterans to just go like that.

David was a young man in the prime of life when he marched away to war, his head filled with legal knowledge and a good deal of religious knowledge, too. He would have made a fine Rabbi, had that been his ambition.

With what sadness we all looked at one another, knowing it was for the best, knowing a huge burden had been lifted from us all. We felt relief; I knew it without others saying it, their eyes and their faces betrayed it – and our guilt for feeling that way, too.

What sadness we had in our lives! It seems we were destined to be forever in mourning for someone, somewhere.

Once again the house was filled with relatives who brought their condolences but their looks which said, 'it had to happen' and 'we knew he would not last' when they knew nothing of the sort. David could have lived a long life sitting by the fire, not moving, for he was a comparatively young man and even the old linger long by the fireside.

And so another body was interred in the unforgiving ground which gave up its clods of earth as if resenting the intrusion of yet another coffin. And we agonised over the words to commemorate the life of a young man who had fought for and been mortally wounded by his own country.

In the end we wrote his name, his years of life and the words Son, Brother and Soldier and left it at that. And we walked away from the stonemasons with heavy hearts for we knew that no words anywhere could describe the life that was David, the golden boy, the sharp mind, the proud body, the patriotism which went bad, the tragedy that was sparked by the results. Could not describe the family hopes and dreams dashed on the rocks of insanity caused by war.

So we were three. Solomon spoke not at all, burying his head at all times in books, the heavier the better it seemed, until they came to rest on the dinner table along with the cutlery. Food was acknowledged with a nod of the head, a wave of the hand, a shadow of a smile which had once crossed that solemn but loving face. Father spoke but in hushed tones as if the dead were lying in a coffin in the next room and should not be disturbed, no matter what. He spoke of the limited orders now coming in to the little shop, of the fact that the others were now getting restless, for profits were small and the work hours long and hard and of the danger which was ever present as they walked the streets of our once proud town.

And the three who had worked together for so long slowly began to drift apart. First the shop next door was closed and the rolls of dark material, holding the dust and hopes of Father and his friends, were brought back into the original shop, still known as The Russian Tailor's, cluttering the shelves, the corridor and the workroom, for there was insufficient money coming in now to rent the two shops. And then one associate said he no longer wished to come to work, fearing for his family and himself and in any event there was little money in it now for them all. Two could divide it better than one. And there were relatives in a safer place –

Father wished him well and said his sad goodbyes.

His remaining associate said he would stay – for now.

We all knew it was the beginning of the end.

The end came sooner than we thought. There were two, then there was one, then there were no orders at all and Father stayed home, sometimes turning the key to the shop over and over in his hands as if it would magic itself into the lock once again, release the darkness which was trapped behind the door, rolled into the dark cloth which still sat there, for no one came any more for suits and coats. No one seemed to have money for such things and if they did they were not spending it.

With rumours rife and death stalking the streets wearing Nazi armbands and speaking with drums and loud music and ranting raving speeches, who had need of suits and coats? Last year's would do for no longer did the men grow stout with good food and the women grow nicely plump with all the rich kosher cooking. Now it was scrabbling for what we could find and what we could eat. Which was not a lot, many times we went hungry.

But we would have been hungrier still had I not learned the lore of the countryside on my solitary walks. For then I knew which berries to pick, which leaves we could eat, where to find mushrooms and nuts and these helped us through the bad times which were around then. It is now, with that wonderful vision we call hindsight, that I know why I was not to play with the boys, why I was left alone and often so lonely for my communion with nature paid off at that time. It has left me with an abiding love for all nature, too. But mostly it was to give us sustenance at that time.

So I walked the fields and pathways, sought the solace of woods and brought home much to eat and much to burn too, so that we could have a small fire and draw something from the sight of the flames and the smell of burning wood, for there is no smell like it on earth. At times, here in the Realms, I catch the scent of wood smoke and I turn to see if I can spy the fire from which it comes, for the flames are givers of light as much as they are of heat. Man is an animal who loves fire. All wild animals run from the flames but those who have been domesticated, the dog, the cat, they seek the fire for its warmth. Man seeks it for light as much as the warmth.

That long winter, the winter of Germany's discontent and our deep and abiding sadness, was hard indeed so the store of wood I brought home during the Autumn was valuable. Where else to store it but in the shop which was not used any more. I used the key, Father would not set foot in there unless he was to work, he said.

So to keep him occupied, for I felt him sliding into a deep well of despair and grief, I asked him to make me a suit.

"Why not?" he said. "The cloth is paid for and is doing nothing." Then he stopped and stared at me for the longest time. I thought he had frozen where he stood, so long did the look go on. Then he burst into tears. He did not put his hands to his face, nor bow his head. He stood, tears bursting from his eyes and streaming down his face as if they would never stop. I said nothing although I wanted to cry out "Father! Please stop!" everything in me said he had to cry this out, whatever sorrow it was.

Finally the tears stopped flowing and then he reached for a handkerchief and dried his face. Then, with shaking hands and quivering lips, he hugged me. Then I began to cry, for I realised Father had never ever hugged me. No touch had come to bind us together. We were strangers, although Father and Son, we were strangers to each other. I cried into the darkness of his suit, having some idea then of why he had cried. His eyes had been opened.

"I have never made you a suit, Daniel."

"No, Father, you never have."

"You never asked for one."

"I had no need of one – until now."

116

"But you have had need! What did you wear for your Bar Mitzvah? What did you wear to funerals? Where have my eyes been that I have not seen these things?"

"I wore Solomon's suit. I wore that which had been given to me."

And it was true. I had no new thing in my entire young life.

"I made Solomon a suit."

"I know."

Father took the key from the hook by the door where I had hung it and went to the shop and there, by lantern light, he cut me a suit. Then he sewed it for me. It took him a week.

Solomon looked surprised when he realised what was happening, the first expression I had seen on his face for the longest time, too.

"So," he said, "there is life in Father yet!"

And he too asked for a new suit. And Father cut and sewed him a new suit, too.

I could not believe the feel of new clothes. Never, in all my years, had I felt anything so wonderful, so crisp and fresh, so – unworn by anyone else. It was entirely unsuitable for just going shopping but I wore it to go shopping just because Father had made it and it was wonderful to wear new clothes. My readers will be astonished at something so trivial meaning so much but when you have had hand-me-downs all your life, something new is something special.

It made the chore of shopping much easier to bear. It also had another effect too: people took me seriously. Before I was just 'the boy' but with a suit on I became a man, growing in stature before their eyes. I was served good quality meat, not the rubbish I had been contending with for weeks, I had good quality vegetables and fruits, such as were available at that time to us Jews, not ones with mould or had been lying around for days in the back of the shop. I was treated differently and I understood for the first time why Father had sewed so many suits for the good burghers of Potsdam and knew too that it was not 'manners maketh man' but 'clothes maketh man.'

Even the Nazi youths, patrolling the streets, throwing refuse and insults in equal measure, held back from shouting at me for a while. For the longest time I believed our problems might be coming to an end, that we might be able to live some kind of normal life because of this, but my hopes and dreams were to be rudely shattered.

Chapter 10

It happened, as such things tend to do, out of the blue one night. We had eaten our meal, had said nothing to one another for there was nothing to be said, but we were sitting in comfortable silence with each other, us three men, lost in our own world of sadness, loss and grief.

So we were sitting when the door was suddenly smashed in and Nazi uniforms filled the space. I could not tell you now of their faces, for they were masks of hatred, not individual people at all. For if they had been individual people, they would have seen us for what we were: one elderly Jewish gentleman – with emphasis on the 'gentle', one scholar and one young man with nothing more in his head than earning a living, sat at a table at which we had consumed a frugal meal and exchanged no words.

"Out!" they shouted and we went, afraid of the guns, afraid of the bullies who had crowded into the small space. Punched, kicked, pushed, we staggered down the stairs where yet more Nazi uniforms waited, their faces equally masked with the same hatred as the ones we heard tearing our small apartment apart above our heads. Father looked up at the ceiling, hearing something break, and said "so this is how it ends." And that was all he said from that moment on.

There are those who, when it was all over, said we should have fought back, that we should not have walked placidly to our trains to take us to our doom. I would say to those people, you were not there. You did not see the masks of hatred, the sheer unbending unbelievable hatred for a fellow human being because he happened to be 'different'. Had Father, Solomon or I fought back at that moment, we would have been clubbed down and kicked to death (it happened to others we heard about) or shot if we had run. And, despite all that came later, when we would wish we *had* done those things so we did not have to endure the unendurable, it is a natural instinct to survive at all costs. For the chance may come in the next five minutes, five hours, five days, five weeks when you could really take a chance and escape.

Nothing was said by any of them. Our names were not mentioned, our destination was a void we were walking into. We saw, when we looked round, that other doors had been smashed in, that other people, neighbours, acquaintances, those we nodded to during the course of a day, were also out in the street surrounded by Nazis. There was a silence above the sound of smashing doors, it was the silence of those who know they have no choice and no words to offer to comfort the other. It was quite clear that had any of us spoken, we would have been knocked down, for the guns were at the ready, the clubs held like guns, they sought only the merest flicker of an eyelid to move.

A poor old man from further along the street shrieked out with pain as he was sent flying into the road. It was like breaking the dam of silence, for the air was suddenly filled with invective, with incoherent shouts of rage and frustration, there were cries of pain, of heart breaking sadness at being dragged from homes we all loved, no matter how mean or bare they were. They represented our roots. We were being torn up by the roots. We stood and we watched as the Nazi thugs kicked the old man in the road, kicked him from one to the other, heard their shouts of laughter as clearly as we heard the breaking bones and when he seemed dead, we were rounded up and marched away. He lay in the road, totally still.

I saw a tear course down Father's face; I saw fear writ large on Solomon's. I know not what expression I carried, for I felt in shock, as if carved from ice, unable to think feel or speak. When jostled by a uniformed arm, I just moved on a little faster.

My memories of that night are of the stars, brilliant points of light, splashed across the night sky in all their cold and unmoving glory. There was no moon, just the coldness of the air around us, for we had no coats, no possessions, no nothing. I remember mourning my new suit which had not been worn enough to be no longer thought of as new. I remember thinking I was glad David was not there, for he would have lost his mind completely to see the way we were being driven, cattle like, toward – what? I remember being glad that Mother was not there to see the destruction of the home she had so loved. And I remember most of all being glad that Rosa was tucked safely into the cold ground, for surely they would have taken her yet again had she lived. It was the first time I had been glad my family were taken from me. It almost lifted my heart for a few moments.

Then I remembered the ones who were left and turned to look for Father and Solomon, finding them a few steps behind me. Solomon tried an encouraging smile but Father was lost, his mind somewhere else. I recognised the look for it was the one David had worn for much of his last year on earth.

The streets were empty of people apart from the group being marched along. Doors were shut and barred, windows curtained and closed against us. No one dared look out. No one dared draw attention to themselves for fear of being part of this terrible parade of human misery.

Past the library where Solomon had spent so much time. Did my brother cast a sad look at it as we passed? I did not dare look. Had Father cast a sad longing look at his shop as we passed? I had not thought to look at that moment. Past the many homes where I had delivered goods for people in the more secure past. Past homes where obviously no one lived any more, for the windows were smashed and the doors stood open. Past a woman wailing her misery to the cold skies and the Nazi men clubbed her and shouted at her to be silent. Had she lost a husband, son, brother, father? Why was she left behind?

And how many women were in this sad parade? Being near the front, I could not see. The tramp of feet on the cold stone, the rustle of clothes as we marched, the occasional shout from one of the Nazis, these sounds stay with me even now.

"So this is how it ends." Father's words seemed to be a fitting epitaph for the Jewish race at that time. That journey's end was the cattle pens at the local station. We were herded in, packed tight, glad of the warmth of the bodies pressed against one another. Outside the pens, armed guards stood with their backs to us, smoking fine cigarettes, passing hip flasks one to the other to ward off the cold, discussing the guarding of such vermin with such hatred that it was a wonder we did not, at that point, join together to overpower them and take our town back. But if we were to speak to one another, to begin the movement to do such a thing, for it could not be done on one person's initiative alone, they would have heard, the guns would have fired and we would have fallen dead there in the pens.

So we stood in the dark, in the cold, in the uncertainty and the fear that uncertainty brings, waiting.

And before long we knew what we were waiting for, from another quarter of Potsdam came another sad parade of men and women, small children, babes in arms.

They were packed into the next pen.

A baby began to squeal as only an infant can. The guard snatched the child from the mother and dashed its brains out against the wall. The mother began to wail and there was a single shot. The sound ceased.

Then we knew we were doomed. We knew what we were up against. We knew that all the rumours we had heard were right. Not just idle talk in the beer houses and shops and clubs, but reality. These men were inhuman, they had no conscience, they had no heart. These men hated the Jews and other 'foreigners' and had declared war on them without it being posted as a declaration of war.

Someone began shouting at us through a loud hailer, telling us we would be moved out as soon as the transport arrived, that a train was coming and we would be put on it, that the town of Potsdam had to be cleansed of our presence. The voice was shrill, verging on the hysterical. When it stopped a silence as thick as the grave itself settled over us. None dared speak. All remembered the child and the single shot.

It was an unnatural silence, for a group of people cannot normally be silent; they will discuss the happening, where they are, what is to happen, how much room they occupy, could someone please move and release their elbow from a stomach or rib, how cold it is, how hungry they are, what they have left behind, what they have seen. We did not speak.

For a long time, too, we did not move. We stood like statues in the pens, frozen to the ground, scared to even look at our neighbour for fear of attracting the wrath of the maniac guards. But slowly someone moved an arm here, a head there, and I found the courage to turn and look at Father and Solomon. Father looked just as blank but Solomon was shocked, it showed in his eyes, his face and his set mouth. It was as if I was his twin at that moment and could receive his thoughts, for I knew what he was thinking.

"For this our brother went to war."

Oh my dear patient reader who has come this far with me, know that now the book is indeed tearing the heart out of me to write! My dear channel has seen me in tears, has held out her arms to me, has offered me her own heart but she knows, as I do, that the story must come from me and from me alone. She does not know what words will come next. She sits, with beautiful music playing through earphones, not listening to anything but the melodies and the words are appearing before her eyes. She feels my pain, she suffers with me. And there are times when I have to tell her we must stop, for I can go no further. And she says, gently, with absolute right on her side, that the sooner we write the book, the sooner my heart will be lighter and freer and I will be able to go forward. I know all this in my mind but my heart is breaking at the memories.

There is no time in the Realms. For me the hurt is as raw as it was that day over 50 years ago. For there is no consolation for those who suffered so much, until they can cleanse themselves of it, which is what I seek to do.

So we are standing in the cold and the dark and the hate and the anger and the fear and the terror in the cattle pen in Potsdam and yet more marching feet are coming, another parade of shambling terrified grief stricken people to join us. And here and there someone cries out as they recognise a face and know that someone else has come to join them in their misery.

And still the train did not come. And of all foolish things, my feet began to ache and I longed to sit down. Standing staring death in the face and my feet ache. It was almost enough to make me smile. But smiling was something I had not done since Mother died and did not expect to do ever again.

There was a commotion behind me, a pushing and a concentrated effort to clear a space. Muttering and cursing followed as we were forced against the rails, shallow breathing as someone leaned against my rib cage. I am not tall, I could not see over the heads of those who clustered around whoever it was who needed the space.

And so I was unaware – until he was carried past me, eyes staring at nothing, face set in the rigidity of the blank mask – that Father had fallen and I had not realised it.

"Is he dead?" someone else asked the question that hovered on my tongue and would not be spoken.

"Yes."

Yes, Father, so this is how it ends. Oh how much suffering you were saved from but how my heart broke as your body went from my sight. I heard one sob, turned to find Solomon, his shocked mask cracked and in pieces, on the verge of breaking down, then the mask was back in place and he looked straight through me as if I, and all the others, did not exist. He had the right idea but it was not something I could do. Then, and now, everything I am and everything I feel is written clear on my face. I can hide nothing. There are many times I have longed for a mask, but never so much as then, that moment, that bitter night in Potsdam.

Bitter is the right word for the way I felt that night! Bitter that we could not, as a people, rise up and crush these oppressors, that we could not drag their guns from their clinging hands and use them on the ugly men with the hateful faces full of hate! Bitter that my country had come to this – on the great international front ready to fight all comers – on the inside fighting all comers by removing those they did not like.

For it was not only Jews herded into those pens that night: there were the disabled, the epileptic, the sick, the coloured skins of the other races.

But revolt, rebellion, call it what you will, was not a part of the equation that night. Shocked people do not combine together to fight back. Shocked people stand with mouths open and hearts sinking to their boots –

Very recently someone close to my channel commented that the heart did not hurt, it was the stomach which hurt. Indeed the words are right, for did my stomach not ache with the pain knifing through it that night! But at the same time, my heart pounded as if it would leap from my body and join poor Father wherever he had gone.

So we stood, with hearts and stomachs dropping to the floor, wondering inside what other terrible atrocities we would witness that night. A bitter wind blew sharp and cold around the buildings, finding our skin, finding our innermost feelings and freezing them. And the clouds built up behind the great wind which blew as if to blow away the hatred and sadness of that terrible night.

So we stood, in darkness, with fear and terror and tears and hearts and stomachs aching and breaking with emotion, waiting for the train to who knew where and to who knew what.

They knew, those who guarded us. We did not know. We could not know, for could anyone in their wildest imaginations understand or appreciate the horror that was ahead? And had we known, would we not have made an effort to snatch those guns and turn them on ourselves after we had shot dead those who persecuted us, just so that we would not have to endure what was ahead?

You have a saying in the modern world: hindsight is 20/20 vision.

We had no idea what was to come.

So we stood and we waited.

And no one spoke.

Not a sound over the whistling of the bitter cold wind around the buildings and the people who stood in the cattle pens. If any cried, they cried silently. If any sobbed, it was deep in the chest where it could not be heard. For we all knew we carried the sorrows of the world on our shoulders, it would not do for one to think he had more sorrow than another so none displayed what they were feeling.

Then the train came. It crawled along the metal road, sparking light into the darkness from its great wheels, steam billowing from its great head, towing cattle trucks behind its great tender. It came to a shrieking halt in front of the cattle pens where we all stood, feeling the heat from the steam and from the boiler. The men who drove the engine were sooty faced and warm, we were white faced and frozen, those of us who had white skins.

The cattle pens were undone, we were ordered to "MOVE!" by the armed guards and we moved as one, a phalanx of bodies surging out into the open space, milling about, stamping feet, flinging arms around ourselves to try and get warm. I turned, looking for Solomon, for my dear serious faced brother, for we had become separated in the crush to leave. I saw him, caught a glimpse of his mask-like face just before the mask snapped again and he rushed forward, snatching a gun from the nearest guard and shooting another in the face and chest before he was mown down in a hail of bullets which took half his immediate neighbours down with him.

I gave one loud cry and was pushed roughly in the back by my nearest neighbour, a dark faced surly man with a huge head of hair.

"Shut up!" he hissed, "do you want to feel the bullets too!"

"But that's my brother ... " I trailed off and allowed myself to be pushed forward into the nearest cattle truck. Brother or father, mother or sister, daughter or son, the relationships no longer mattered in a world gone mad. The pain was so great I was numb. First Father, then Solomon, gone in a short time, away from the horror of all this madness, this insanity, this world which had stood itself on its head. Solomon, who was going to be the greatest professor of history Germany had ever had was now part of its history, a statistic in the bloody war ranged against us Jews.

Standing in the corner of the cattle truck, sheltered at least from the bitter wind, crushed against the man who had shut up my outburst and perhaps saved my life, I mourned … for the suit Father had made and I had not worn enough times to make shabby, to lose its new smart feeling, for the way the suit made me feel, for the joy I felt whenever I slipped it on. I mourned for a suit.

The guilt I felt when I realised where my mind had gone was overwhelming, it almost crushed me completely. Darkness actually swept over me for a while and I knew nothing until I came to my senses later, realising by the jolting and rattling that we were on the move.

The rational part of me, the Daniel which lived quietly in there and who was responsible for the calculated moves I made, said had I mourned for my brother and father, my mind would have cracked under the weight of the sorrow. The rational side of me said that was why I mourned for something as materialistic as a suit. The emotional side of me said 'but you mourned for a suit not for your much loved brother and father!' and the guilt surged in again.

So, as we rattled our way across Germany to who knew where and to who knew what, we cried and sobbed, we coughed and spat, we urinated out of the partly open door when the need was so great, those of us who could, the others did it where they stood and we all had to bear it for none could move out of the way to allow a neighbour the chance to do such a thing.

And we died. Some of us died. Some of us had heart conditions that would not withstand a standing journey crushed in like cattle into freezing cold trucks, some of us were weighed down by sorrow to the point when we did not wish to carry on. The murmur would go round that another had 'gone' and we would try and shift a half inch, a mere fraction, to make a space for the body to be moved, a little at a time, until it reached the door when, with a brief prayer, it was launched into the darkness. And we all breathed a little easier for there was a little more space now to stand, move even, flex the arms and legs, turn around and look at another neighbour, seeking a friendly face, or even a familiar one.

I knew no one. And, by the lack of recognition, no one knew me, either.

My neighbour who had saved me spoke softly in my ear when he could.

"My friend, you almost died back there. Maybe it would have been better for you to have joined your brother but I feel it was not your time. It was his time. You are young. You are strong. You might yet survive that which is ahead of us."

"I thank you for what you did. It was a moment of impulse, for I loved my brother so."

"Do we not all love our brothers and our families, and are we not split wide apart by the madness which is abroad in this fair land of ours?"

At that moment another body was edging its sad way to the door. This time, in defiance perhaps, or out of a deep need, my new-found friend began a loud and emphatic chanting of the Prayer for the Dead.

Wholeheartedly everyone joined in, so that the sound could be heard above the clanking of the wheels, the rattling of the truck, the clinking of the chains and hooks holding the trucks to one another. And as we did this, we heard another chant set up from the next truck, joining ours, and yet another. While we could not hear further than that, we had no doubt that all the trucks were joining in and so the prayer was repeated and repeated like a mantra, lifting our spirits out of the blackness and into the light where a benign and great

God might interfere, stretch out a great hand and lift his Chosen People from the terrible pit of Hell in which they found themselves.

Nothing happened like that but we did actually smile at one another, something we saw when the bitter moon shone into the truck from time to time.

And the trucks rolled on in the night.

And the bodies were committed to the railway embankments.

And we had space to breathe and even, toward the end of the night, to sit. That is, if we did not mind sitting in the pools of urine which had run down the legs of the women or been directed at the floor by the men who could not reach the door in the early hours of our journeying but who now could and did stand in the doorway and spray the passing grass with their fluids.

Looking back, I wonder that there was no speech between us. Were we all sunk so deep into our terrors, our horrors, our personal hells, that we could not express a word of sympathy and support with one another? After we all chanted the Prayer For the Dead as we did, until our voices cracked with the strain, we went silent again, silent into the rolling darkness of the unknown.

I know I was numb with grief, there was no feeling inside, just a cold block of stone which pumped blood whether I wanted it to or not. I knew I was in need of food for the stomach said it was empty and the throat said it would like a drink but nothing was there for us, for any of us. I knew I was in need of a long time of crying but the tears were all dried up and hidden behind the mask I adopted after my dear brother broke his and dropped down into the mud and dirt of Potsdam.

When the sky streaked red with a dawn that was welcome only in that we could now see a little more, the train began slowing down. We were in a suburbs somewhere, shabby warehouses and stores, some rusting cars and broken down lorries. We saw no people apart from the guards who suddenly appeared alongside the train, guns at the ready, daring us to make a move to escape. Shocked and exhausted as we were, none of us were in a fit state to try and make a run for it. We knew we could not outrun a bullet.

Civilians came alongside, too, handing up loaves of stale bread and canisters of water which we took and broke up and shared between us. The guards joked among themselves about how many were left after the long night, how many had not made the journey so far, as if it was a competition to see who could survive to the end of the line – wherever that was.

"At least the ones who are left will be fit to work," said one, menacing us with a gun as he spoke. "We need workers at the camp."

It was the first time we had an indication of where we were going. A camp. I saw faces lighting up. A camp could mean food and shelter, something to do, some useful work, a reason to carry on living until this whole stupid nonsense sorted itself out.

But inside I stayed cold. Nothing a Nazi said to a Jew could be good, no matter what it sounded like on the surface. The camp could be nothing like the image which sprung to mind immediately. It could be something else and what work could a Jew do for a Nazi, I asked myself. I had no answer but I did not like the thought.

With a jolt and a clanging of metal and shouts of encouragement, the train began to pick up speed again and rattled its way through desolate countryside. Had there been bombing, or a fire? Everything looked wasted, destroyed; the few people we glimpsed were cowed, bowed down by trials perhaps beyond those we were suffering. Even accepting the fact it was winter and the trees were empty of covering, it still seemed desolate out there.

It was desolate in the truck, too, for it grew colder as the day went on and there were fewer of us to keep each other warm. Someone pulled the door shut so we could not see the devastation outside and to keep the coldness out. It was darker like that but we had nothing to see but one another anyway so it did not matter. We stood back to back and front to front, sometimes a hand on an arm or round a shoulder, sometimes we hugged, sometimes we just stood, but at no time did we speak. Sometimes we stood and let the tears pour down our faces with our grief but no sound ever came. Everything was done silently. For we were a silent people in that time of woe. Gone were the days when our leader Moses shouted the Ten Commandments to the people, since Gideon shouted with trumpets at the walls of Jericho and brought them down. Gone were the days when we Jews were prepared to announce ourselves to the rest of the world. A proud people, reduced to huddling for comfort in a railway truck, turned out of our homes, our villages, our towns and our lives by others stronger and more violent than ourselves, those with hatred in their hearts for people they perceived unclean and different.

And in the darkness of that night I truly believed God had forsaken His Chosen People.

Chapter 11

The train came to a juddering halt, throwing us here and there, on top of one another, crashing into walls and the floor. How grateful we were at that moment that the doors had been closed for surely we would have been thrown clear of the truck. There was the most awful grinding crunching noise which seemed to come from way ahead of us.

Then we heard the guards, "Out! Out! Form a line! March!"

We climbed out, helping the weaker ones, lifting the women down to avoid them exposing their legs to the waiting German guards. For a fleeting moment I held a woman in my arms and realised, with a pain that was almost as deep as that which knifed through me when my beloved brother was shot down that I had missed out on the feminine softness a woman could give. The last few years before this terrible time had been a time of men, the occasional aunt had hugged and kissed but they were not 'women', they were relatives and one did not cling to them as I suddenly wished to cling to the woman I was helping. But I let her go, for I did not know her and she did not know me and the proprieties had to be observed even at this time. For what was life without its social structure?

It was early in the morning, the sun was streaking the cold sky with red fingers. There were black clouds building up, ominous in their heaviness. But we had to look forward, not up. Forward to the place where we were going.

We marched, two abreast, down the side of the train which we soon found had stopped because the engine had left the rails. We were in deep countryside, stark trees, cold bitten earth, no one to see us. If ever a

133

derailment was in an opportune place for escape, this was it. But the guards held their rifles at the ready and watched every move. We did not dare make the break. At least, those of us who had a guard within eyesight did not dare make a break. I heard at least one shot but have no way of knowing if anyone did escape, for we could not look round, we were snarled at if we did.

We walked. We walked down the side of the track, seeing the rails glimmering silver in the early morning light, seeing the dawn through the branches, seeing no chance of freedom. A loaf of bread was passed back along the line, we broke some off and handed it on. Another loaf was passed along, this was not broken until it reached those behind us, for there was not enough in one loaf to feed all the people who had survived the journey so far.

That was not knowledge; that was assumption. If you have trucks full of people crammed in together and in one people die on the journey, it is reasonable to assume that the people died in the other trucks, too.

We were a sad group making our way along the railway line. We were sad, it showed in the stoop of shoulders, the weary tread, the silence apart from the sound of feet on gravel. We were going to an unknown destination and would be walking for an unknown length of time. Despair dragged at my heart and mind, I wanted to run from the column of people, knowing that a bullet would end the misery there and then.

I wanted to but the desire to live was stronger than the desire to end it all. The saying 'where there's life, there's hope' is a truism which takes many people through many difficult times. We did not know where we were going, we had no way of knowing what was ahead of us. It could be better than we feared, or worse than we hoped, but until we got there, we had to walk in some degree of hope.

But the walk took its toll of some people. I saw people detouring, stepping over the line perhaps and wondered why they did it. Then I got to that point and would see that someone had either fallen down and died or lain down and died. Their faces were frozen in the despair we all felt, for sure. It happened more and more as the day wore on and we got more and more weary and despairing.

Just when it was all getting too much for us, we were ordered to halt. We sat on the embankment, staring at the empty rails, wondering what it was all about.

After a rest of quite some time, we heard the rails humming and a train appeared, drawing to a halt alongside us. I do not know if it was the same engine or another one, all engines look the same to me but it pulled trucks similar to those we had travelled in. These were full of despairing people who stood back to make room for us to clamber on board, again helping the women so they did not reveal themselves to lustful German eyes.

The Jews on board this train had recently been given a bread ration. They shared it with us.

The strange thing is, these people were the same as we had been. Not a word spoken, just a wordless handing over of bread, a consoling hug, a sympathising look. They too wore the stains of tears freely shed during the night. They too stood in puddles of urine where they had not been able to deal with bodily functions any other way. They too had the same look of despair stamped into them. It was as if the Germans had ordered up an identical set of Jews to send to wherever we were going and these were clones of ourselves.

They weren't clones, they were individuals, with heartbreak and sorrow weighing them down, even as we were. Once inside the truck, gaining warmth from the bodies once more, we became one, another cohesive unit travelling to their/our fate.

I did not know at this time but found out later, from talking with others, that the reason we travelled so long and so far and so dismally was so that we would not know where we were going and that others could not trace where we were going. For surely Germany is not that big that we should be travelling for so long! But diverted here and there, sent down this line and another, to confuse, to disorientate, to camouflage, this was the reasoning. If you can call it that.

And so, by devious and diverse routes, we came to our destination.

There has been a gap of some 48 earthly hours between the writing of the last line and the beginning of this section, 48 hours in which my channel has gone about her daily life, attended a meeting and worked on other things. But I am aware that at no time have her thoughts left the subject to which we are heading, as inexorably as the train carried us there. Her pain is already in place, before we reach our destination, pain she is picking up from me and from which I cannot protect her, no matter how much I would like to do so. To open oneself to Spirit in this way is to receive and share the pain the subject must of itself bring to those who are sensitive as she is.

So, to spare her the pain as much as I can, we must push onward, despite the reluctance on my part to venture into this section of the book.

There were high walls. There were watchtowers. There were guards. There was barbed wire and there were dogs.

In no way could anyone believe we were entering a place of work. We were entering a prison camp.

If we had low spirits before, on our endless soul destroying journey, we had a greater depth of spirits now, they plummeted and went on plummeting until they reached the ground and then went right on dropping until I felt I was completely empty, drained of all emotion and feeling of any kind.

For here was hate writ large on the face of the fair land once known as Germany. Why did they need high walls, watchtowers, guards, barbed wire and dogs for a few homeless displaced Jews, we asked ourselves. We? We talked of such things later, when the darkness fell and the guards were not so worried about rebellion or mutiny. We talked and we knew we all felt the same.

But we were not to know that – I was not to know that when, as a young man, I walked from the train under the sight of the guards and their guns, through the great gates and into a living Hell.

Segregation first, women into one line, men to another. Husbands and wives clung together, were torn apart. Children were sent into another line, screaming and crying for their parents. Beaten with sticks, cursed, kicked and spat at, we were ordered into huts where our clothes were taken from us and we were pushed, naked, before a man in a white coat who looked us over, got us to turn around, asked our age and wrote something on a list. The older men, the sick ones, were shuffled off through one door. The stronger younger ones were directed through another door. Even as we walked through, we heard the sound of gunfire and knew, without being told, that the old and the sick were no more.

In the next room were more men and a nurse. She did nothing but look at us with utter contempt and loathing. For were we not shrivelled unimposing specimens, castrated through terror and cold, into not very inspiring human beings? Was it our fault?

It was here we were given the number – given because we never fought, we took it. I have it still. I will not lose it, even in the Realms, for it is a mark of my last incarnation and I wish to retain it. It was here we were given the 'uniform' of the convict, the shapeless garment which covered but did not warm, retained modesty but did nothing for the self-image, for we were all the same. And our heads were shaved.

And we were pushed out into the compound where there were many, many others all wearing the same uniform, all with shaved heads, some with stick-like arms and skeletal bodies.

It was a place of death. Of walking dead.

My tears dried up in that moment.

My tears stayed dried up for the remainder of my earthly existence.

I have cried them since, in the Realms, where there are comforting arms and understanding souls but at that time, in the harshness of the reality which faced me, there was no room, no time, no place for tears.

We were given a number and pointed in the direction of a hut. There we, those who travelled the same Via Dolorosa with me, found the shelves which were our bunks. Found the lack of warmth and comfort, found there was nothing but survival at the heart of everything.

On that first day we were left alone. Men mourned the loss of their wives, not knowing where they were, what they were enduring, were they too wearing the same shaming garment and had the same shaming head shaving, for a woman to lose her hair is so very shaming and degrading. And the children, where were they and what were they feeling, how alone, how lonely and lost they must be! So we talked in low voices of that which hurt us so much, of the despair which haunted us, which already marked our eyes and our faces, for we knew, without being told, that there was no way out of here except through death's own savage door and where would that take us?

And as we talked so we became more bitter and hurt and one man began keening, a terrible sound that tore at the soul and the heart, so we silenced him with our hands and our arms and our fears for we did not wish to bring down the wrath of the guards so soon after we had arrived.

Later in the day a small bread ration was issued and with that we climbed onto our bunks and tried to get some sleep, not knowing what the morning would bring.

But what sleep could a body find on hard planks, with nothing but a worn out blanket for cover or pillow, time spent debating what was the best use of the miserable piece of material supplied, ears besieged with the coughing, shuffling, talking, moaning, keening, whining, grumbling people sharing the hut with you? I swear I did not sleep that night. The thoughts tormented, the number burned itself into my skin and my mind, the shameful number which made me nothing more than an item, a mere commodity to be disposed of as they wished; the grief haunted me, the loss of family, friends, those whom I had known briefly, those I had seen but once, those who had shared the terrible everlasting train journey with me who I would never see again, for they littered the countryside along the railway lines. I wanted to weep for those who had no grave. But the tears had dried, as I said before, there were no tears.

For the sake of peace of mind for those of my readers who are or likely to be tormented by thoughts of those bodies along the side of the railway lines, let me say here that since I reached the Realms and made enquiries and was sought out by those who knew of such things, I have been assured that the villagers rescued all the bodies and gave them a quiet solemn burial. These Christian people buried the Jews with reverence and dignity and it is good to know that the resting places were hallowed by villagers, who went to great lengths to do this Christian duty to fellow men and women. The graves remain unmarked but untouched. The sanctity of the dead is preserved.

I also know that the shell we leave behind is no more than a shell, that we should not concern ourselves with the material body which we once inhabited, but old habits die very hard and we do care about our earthly remains. Those who were spared the terrible ordeals that were in the future for us were glad to know that their earthly remains were in sacred ground, no matter that they were not buried with all the due reverence and solemnity of Jewish law.

But lying awake on hard planks, in the overheated, foetid hut crowded with the flotsam and jetsam of the Jewish race, those who had been swept up and deposited here by the All Powerful Germans with the terrible SS insignia on their sleeves, I did not know of these things and I mourned their passing and their unseemly resting places. People I did not know, people I would never know, had passed from my life to the next in a way that seemed terrible to me – then.

The night seemed endless. The hours dragged their feet, what hours there were for without watches or time pieces of any kind, without sight of moon or stars, how could we know the passing of time? But it was an endless time of subdued noise, of quiet tears, of the occasional sob or heart-breaking groan of pure pain and suffering, of shuffling bodies as people moved and tried to find rest. Some shuffled to the corner to deposit urine and other bodily functions, adding to the smell which permeated the whole place. Someone was sick. I swear I smelled blood.

The night might have seemed endless but the raucous shouts which roused the 'sleeping' people as the first light touched the daylight hours was even more unwelcome. We were hustled out to stand in ragged freezing lines for 'roll call' and it was then the true horror began to sink in. For the dead were laid out alongside the living, so the roll call could be made. And the dead were taken and stacked to one side.

Thin gruel was handed out for us to eat and then we were detailed, some of us, to become work units, issued with spades and told to march. With our ragged clothes and our shabby boots we must have looked a sight fit for something from a horror film, but a horror film has an orchestrated theme, a director and many, many film crew. Here the horror film had no orchestrated theme, apart from degradation, humiliation and death, the director was the Chancellor himself and the film crew walked in thick warm uniforms and held guns at the ready.

We were set to work digging.

Digging graves. Digging long trenches to be used as graves.

As we dug, we realised some of us were being watched more closely than others. I say we at this time, for it was discussed later and I found we all saw and felt the same thing. In adversity, people do come together in mind body and spirit, so it was a collective thing in any event. After we had dug and dug for what seemed like ages, with shouts of encouragement and abuse from our guards, who lolled under trees with flasks of spirits or something being passed from hand to hand, we were segregated. Some were pushed to one side, under guard, the others ordered to stand where they had been digging. Their spades were taken away and then one by one they were shot in the back of the head, so they fell face forward into the hole they had dug.

And I stood in total shock and horror, speechless, incapable of movement until someone shoved me roughly in the back and made me move, and it was then I realised that the guards were shouting at us to March on! March on! March on back to the camp.

And as we marched on, we passed a detail of prisoners carrying the dead to the trench we had just dug.

Chapter 12

The first few days I spent at that camp were the most awful days of my life. I did not believe anything could be worse than what I had already endured but this was definitely the worst of all. It was inconceivable to my young mind that human beings could treat other human beings in such a fashion, treat them as if they were lower than cattle, for the way we were herded, fed, kept in huts on benches, was not the way anyone kept animals in that time. In fact, it was the forerunner of what you know now as battery farming. Crushed into one small space, fed virtually nothing, set to labour on so many tasks: sorting the clothes from the living, the gold teeth and other priceless items from the dead, even taking the skin to use for lamps. And that has been mentioned in other books which have detailed the horrors of the concentration camps, but I saw it happen.

And every morning there were the deaths. Every morning were the roll calls, the shivering trembling terrified people standing in rows in their 'convict outfit' which is how I thought of it and always will, with the dead laid out neatly in rows to ensure the count was right.

Every night the senselessness of where we were, what we were forced into doing, the bitterness, the burning hatred, the anxiety for our loved ones (those who still had loved ones alive somewhere in this camp or elsewhere in the battered land of Germany) became too much and a heart would stop somewhere during the dark hours of agony and desperation. And those who were left would envy those who had left this world, for their suffering was at an end we who were left had to carry on.

Many times during those first few days I wanted to die. Wanted to run at the wire and electrocute myself, run at the guards and be shot, try to escape and be shot. Wanted not to eat and to starve to death. Wanted to ask someone to smother me and put me out of my misery.

I did none of those things. In the long dark bitterness of the night, when the hut came alive with moans, groans, creaks and cries, with tears and keening sadness, I discovered a faith I did not know I had.

It seems an awful place to say I found God. Awful because it seems as if I reached out in my extreme agony, when I cared not for Him when living my other life. So it seemed to me at first, until I turned my thoughts inward to that other life.

Now that I am strong enough to write of these things I can go back – as it were – to talk of things in my childhood I could not bring myself to write when we were at that part of the book.

Let me explain. When this book began, in the summer of 1998, there were occasions when all I could write was one or two lines. At most we achieved a paragraph, my channel and I, then I would stop and tell her I could not go on. The book progressed so very slowly, a little here, a little there: I had my problems, my channel had hers, for she had a life to lead at that time – and still does! – and we were writing of things which were agonising to me: the death of my beloved grandfather, my relatives, my sister, my brother's experiences in the war and the after effects, it was all too much for me at that time. So I kept the writing to that which mattered at that time.

Now I am stronger, for I have drawn some powerful friends to me to help me with this part of the book, I can go back and write of that which was left out at that time.

Forgive me, dear reader, for a diversion. It is necessary, it is essential! I told my channel it would be a purge and so it will, for I have to write of this to release my mind and my heart of its burdens.

You will recall, dear reader, that my childhood was not a happy one. I was a lonely boy, never chosen for the games in the street, always seemingly left out by my siblings, the twins had each other and David was just too old, too big and too experienced to spend time with a little one like me.

Now I can add the part which I missed out then.

My father was a sadist.

On many occasions he struck my dear mother in his temper, would flare up at the smallest thing out of place or said out of line. His grief at her passing was as much guilt as bereavement. The twins escaped his wrath mostly but even they suffered at his hands, cruel hands which would lash out and crack a head against a wall or make a nose bleed with a face slap, from time to time. We walked and lived in awe of our father.

I do not believe I was a wanted child. I believe I was what is known as an 'accident', a non-planned baby. I may be wrong and one day I will find out if I am wrong, when I finally sit down and talk with my mother. I have not done this yet for I have had to clear my mind of this huge burden of sorrow and resentment, its bitterness and sadness have been like a canker eating away at my insides for too long. I could not sit with someone and talk of such things without it bursting out and that would not do in the Realms. So that reconciliation is for later, when the book is done. But it seemed to me I was an unwanted child, why else should I warrant such extreme danger from my father who should, by all natural laws, have just loved me?

He would beat me. He wore a leather belt which he used on my back, my buttocks, my legs, even my arms at times. I wore bruises as others wore a sun-tan. I hid them from Mother and from my siblings, for I believed it was a fault in me which made Father beat me so hard and so often.

Mother did not know. Father would come and stand at the door and crook a finger at me and I would leave what I was doing and follow him. We would go to the shop when no one was there and I would lean over the dark rolls of cloth and he would beat me until his temper was gone.

I said in earlier pages that the dark rolls of cloth absorbed many a tear. They certainly absorbed a lot of mine.

There, it is said. I have said it. A burden has just rolled from me as it did to Christian in that old book, the Pilgrim's Progress. It has rolled down the hill and burst into a thousand pieces all over the world. My tears are gone with it.

So, add the pain of the suffering to the loneliness, the 'left out' feeling, the tragedies which struck us, one after the other, and ask yourself why I did not turn to God at any time back then but came to Him in the hut in a concentration camp deep in the German countryside and I have no answer for you.

I tell you these things so you will see that the faith which I found then was based on real love for my creator, not just on a 'get me out of this' desire for help, for life had been bad enough before to warrant asking for the helping hand of an all-powerful God but I never did.

And much of this came from the hypocritical families around us at that time. We knew, of course we did, of those who abused their children, those who used their children in ways it was not natural to do and those same people donned their best clothes and went to the synagogue to pray every holy day and Sabbath and had the rabbi call on them and observed the ordinances and holy day rituals. They were the ones with the candles in the window and the strictness of the Black Fast and all to show us how good they were. And I knew then that was not the God I wanted to have in my life, one who could look down on such people and reward them with yet more money or a better position.

But when I came to Him, in the darkest hours of the morning, just before dawn, when I finally opened my heart and said: "I am yours, great God," much became clear to me. God is all-powerful, all-seeing, all-loving but He gave us freewill. He does not demand we love him, He asks but that is not demanding. He sees that we offend and sees too that sometimes it is because we are weak in our hearts and our minds. He does not interfere. He does not give this one a better position than another, or more money, or anything else which makes that person richer than the next, that is a man-made thing. Money does not come from God.

There is much I could say on this subject, but it is not the time nor the place: these are merely the very edges of my reasoning. But finding God meant I could not run to the wire, try to escape or attack a guard or do anything which would end my life and take away my suffering, for I wanted some time to explore this God-Daniel relationship a little further before deciding what was best for me. And what He wanted for me.

So I spent my nights, when not lost in deep, exhausted slumber, offering up prayers to my God. Silent prayers, for there were others who shouted aloud to their Creator and were scorned by many who said God had forsaken His people in their time of great suffering. And I knew even then, without the benefit of much religious education or much reading on the subject, that the suffering of His people was damaging to God's heart at that time – but He could not interfere. How could He? Was He to reach down with a great hand and take away the concentration camps? What of all the people who would be left? Where would they go, what would they do? And if you started such a thing, where did it stop? What about every prison in every land, what about the

146

killing which went on in all the other lands around this globe of ours? And if God got involved and stopped every war, every terrorist group, every dictator, what would people say? Would they not say, 'why did he not stop that car killing my child?' and 'why was my mother taken in such a terrible disease ridden way, why wasn't she saved?' and where would it all end?

God gave us freewill. Hitler and his cohorts used theirs to build camps and inter thousands of people for no reason that I could see then – or now. Father used his to abuse his youngest son and exert his authority over his family at all times. David used his to stop his own heart when the Nazi brigade began tramping through Potsdam.

I once said in a communication to a Circle, to a group of light minded loving people that I would not give philosophy; that was not my role in life. I now find I am giving philosophy both in Circle and here in my own book, but these are things I feel I must say.

My channel, before she knew me, once wrote to a correspondent that the Jews do not have a monopoly on suffering and she was right. Mayan culture, Inca culture, they destroyed themselves and the Spanish came and finished off the job. Long before the Second World War began, the Australian people wiped out the Tasmanians. The Americans have done their best to eliminate their native neighbours. Since the Second World War, Cambodia has seen the Killing Fields and Vietnam has torn itself apart and had to rebuild. Korea is a divided country with families divided for the same length of time I have been in the realms searching for my own saviour. Uganda, South Africa, Zimbabwe, how many countries do we need to name to say that the Jews do not have a monopoly on suffering? And as we write this book, my channel and I, so Israel/Palestine is once again in conflict, with people being torn apart by hatred, by religion, by the greed and need for land of their own.

And as we write this part of the book, my channel and I, so we approach yet another Armistice Day when you remember the dead of many wars. My channel will sit and her heart will weep tears of blood when the petals cascade from the roof of the Albert Hall, one for every soul lost in the conflicts which tore apart a whole continent.

No, the Jews do not have a monopoly on suffering, but at the height of the Second World War, it seemed as if we did, for we saw no release, no end to the misery in which we were kept and no end to the uses they made of us.

If life in the camp can ever be said to be 'normal', it seemed that way for a few weeks after we arrived. The roll call each morning, the work, building, digging, transporting, the lack of food, the lack of comfort, all became something to be accepted, endured, coped with. Each of us learned who to avoid, who was in the pockets of the Nazis, who was likely to 'tell' on you for any reason and earn that person a savage beating in front of the silent lines in the morning. Beaten for taking an extra scrap of food, foraging for something to wear in the coldness, slacking on a job, talking out of turn about the German regime, anything and everything, it seemed, could get you into trouble with the Authorities.

I saw many such beatings, saw how they – the guards, the trusties, whoever – delighted in what they were doing, took real joy in inflicting savage pain on another human being. They broke arms, broke legs, broke ribs, cracked skulls, left people lying in the mud and the cold to die. And none of us dared go near them. Only once someone tried and was beaten to death because of it. After that no one dared.

It is in the heart of every man to go and help another, it is not natural to walk by and leave someone there but it was something we had to do. And it broke my heart to do it.

We were many people in the camp; we were men, women and children of all ages. We were pushed together in work and in sleep, in fighting for food and in keeping warm. Sometimes we exchanged names, usually we did not for it was not good to get close to someone, only to watch them die the next morning for some 'indiscretion' or other. We referred to each other by the last digits of our hated numbers, if we did it at all.

We grew thinner and thinner. Clothes hung on us, we were walking skeletons labouring for the well fed well clothed German soldiers sent to guard us and kill us, if they so chose. It seemed no one cared, no one was prosecuted for abusing the prisoners.

I said the word. I said the word which earlier held me back from pushing ever onward with this wretched book, as I have come to think of it, and even now I know I can do no more this night for the word has aroused great emotion and it is time to stop. But I know where I must go tomorrow in this sad story and my channel knows, too. She will thus be prepared for what is to come.

Chapter 13

Abuse. When you hear or read the word, what do you imagine? Sexual or physical abuse? In the camp we suffered both. Mental abuse came with the stench of unwashed bodies crammed into huts, with the smell of the lime sprinkled on the dead in their trenches, or the odd whiffs of gas we experienced from time to time until we realised what it was – the terrible gas chambers where prisoners were marched in to 'shower' and never came out alive again. They 'showered' those who were not wanted any more, the sick, the infirm, the ugly, anyone they did not like. Children who did not co-operate were sent along to the 'showers' and we heard the screams above the sound of the beating of our own hearts and the shouts of the guards and the barking of the dogs kept to chase those who tried to escape. We heard the screams and we held ourselves tight with rage, hatred and fear. Who knew who would walk into the chambers next?

Abuse. Mental abuse was something which drove many over the edge into insanity and were thus picked out for the chambers immediately. Insanity was something the Germans feared, it was like an illness to them, they disposed of them very quickly indeed. Show signs of being mentally unbalanced and you signed your own death warrant immediately. But who could not go insane, living on the edge of starvation, of the edge of death, day and night? Who would not go insane, knowing their loved ones could be next to take the walk of death, or be clubbed down by the sadistic guards and trusties or earmarked for –

Who would not go insane just to be out of the nightmare that was the camp where we were held? The nightmare was compounded by the fact we knew we were not alone in our camp, that there were others just like it, with the same regime in place and the same aim, to dispose of the Jews once and for all.

There were ever flickers of hope. New arrivals would have caught some item of news somewhere, we knew that the armies of Britain, France, Belgium and others had risen up against the invaders, that there were Resistance workers fighting to disrupt the advance of the German Army across Europe, that there was bombing of the great German cities by the RAF. We knew it but somehow it made no impression on us, for we believed that we were doomed and that all the bombing in the world would not rescue us from our fate.

And still I walk away from the subject!

I must force myself, for the whole point of this book is to tell the truth.

I visited my channel when she sat in Circle one night to have a conversation with her and with those who sat with her. And she said she had come across the text which said: "Ye shall know the truth and the truth shall set you free."

So it will. I shall be free of all that is holding me to the earth plane when I can bring myself to finally write this book to its bitter end and release my mind and soul from its sorrows of this last reincarnation.

Physical abuse. We were punched, kicked, beaten with clubs, with sticks, with the butt of guns, for nothing more than looking in the wrong direction at the wrong time. We were often beaten down to the earth simply because someone wanted to do it. You cannot understand how a race of people could be so violent, so unbelievably cruel, to fellow human beings, fellow Germans.

And I have to make a stand here and say something that will upset a lot of people, but as I said and my channel said, 'ye shall know the truth and the truth shall set you free'. This is a truth that is unpalatable to many, even to me as I write of it. I may use another's hands but the writing is mine, for my channel does not write like this, her own work is entirely different. She knows that, she knows that this is not her imagination!

Some who beat us to the ground were British officers.

Not all the soldiers and airman who were captured by the Germans ended up in Colditz and places like that, from which they made their heroic escapes. Some were brought to the camps, because they were nearer and more convenient for retaining prisoners of war. We were considered prisoners of war, even as they practised extermination on us; we were still referred to as prisoners of war. For what war did we fight, I wondered?

And those who were brought to the camps were revered by the guards for they were officers, even if they were of 'the enemy'. And they were given clubs and sticks and strutted around the camp as if they owned it. They had more food than us, they looked at us with the same hatred and contempt that the German guards did, we read it in their faces and in their eyes.

They had a separate hut, warmer than ours, where they congregated of an evening. And if they wanted a diversion, they would send out for a woman, or several women, or lots of women. And we would hear the sounds of the abuse, hear the rapes which went on, the screaming women, the sounds of lust, the cheering on of each other. We heard the sounds and we shivered in the darkness and in the cold and sobbed silently for our women were being desecrated by these animals.

Sometimes the women came back to the hut, bleeding from the wounds inflicted by these men. Sometimes the women came back to the hut bleeding, for they had their monthly problems and it had made no difference to the men who took them carnally. Sometimes the women did not come back to the hut and then there would be a keening sadness running through us all as a bunk remained empty.

But not for long, for there was always a new consignment of prisoners of war arriving by foot, hopeless, helpless, lost and deprived of all hope, shovelled in through the gates with their barbed wire and guards and dogs, lost before they came, lost when they came, certainly lost when they saw the walking skeletons who were the occupants of the camp.

But what could you do when guards with guns came to the door and shouted 'You, you and you!' pointing to the women they had picked out for the night? If anyone dared call out after them as they walked out of the door, some proud with their heads held high, some with stooped shoulders and lowered head, if anyone dared call encouragement or strength or anything at all, that person would be dragged from their bunk and clubbed to the ground.

So the poor helpless doomed women would walk out in silence, knowing we dared not speak. They had no chance to say goodbye, to wish anyone luck in the future, they just walked out and sometimes they never came back.

Those who did would sometimes wish they had not come back.

One woman, who had been taken in every orifice over and over again during the course of one long agonising night, and who came back pouring blood from her mouth, nose and ears, as well as from her bodily openings, said nothing to us. She stood and let us see her in all her bloody glory, then she turned and walked to the wire where she was shot. They left her body there all day as a lesson to us all.

We needed no lesson.

We knew all we needed to know from her appearance when she came back to the hut that night.

And when they got tired of choosing women for their fun – they began on the children.

Now it is my channel who hesitates, not I! For this goes deep into her soul and as she writes this she has tears.

I am sorry, my dear sister, but the truth will set me free and you know it, so be brave for me and write these words.

Children. Girls of 8 and 9 and 10 were taken from their beds to the hut of the officers and to the huts of the guards, too.

Boys of 8 and 9 and 10 were taken from their beds to the hut of the officers and to the huts of the guards, too, for those who preferred to take their sex that way. Broken bleeding shattered bodies were returned in the morning for us to carry to the trenches to bury, covered in lime, and covered in our tears. Well, some could still cry but as I said before, my tears had dried and would not be shed. They remained as a lump somewhere in my chest, hurting me, but I could not release them. I never did release them.

It was this outrage which made me try my escape. My first escape.

I watched the guards, timed their patrols, saw where there was a chance to make it under the wire and out into the surrounding woods. Spring was coming, there were buds on the trees and some leaves on bushes and there might be a little cover for a convict on the run. I told no one of my plan for talk was dangerous. We had all learned the art of silence, that silence is truly golden if it means your life is to be preserved.

I watched and waited for what felt like forever but was probably about a week, although we had no way of regulating the days of the week. I had no idea how long I had been in the camp or what month it was. We only knew it was Spring by the trees and plants outside the camp. There were none inside.

And while I watched and waited, the officers and the guards began a new game. Torture. Tired of rape and sodomy, they began playing games with the prisoners, nailing them to doors to see how long they would last, burning them with coals, beating them, knocking out their teeth, blinding them – if I was to recite every torture it would make a book so horrific none would wish to buy it. Even more horrific than the story I already tell and that is bad enough. So I will desist but you get the general idea. There was so much agony, so much suffering, so much pain and death that went on inside the camps, apart from the walks to the gas chambers! There have been books written about the camps, about the regime, about the medical experiments and the terrible things which went on. If you really must read more, go and find the books, for they will tell you so much more than I can. I will bring you my truth, for my truth will set me free. This is the life Daniel led in the prisoner of war camp. This is the truth that Daniel brings to you from the Realms through the hands of a willing, devoted and loving channel who is moved to tears by the words she is writing now, at this point of the book. Her sorrow is my balm, for I know she would not cry if she did not care, did not feel deeply about the subject and about the man who is writing it. Forgive me, sister, but the words must be said.

I was not strong. I was not entirely weak yet, but not strong yet I knew I had to try and escape. Others had tried: some had made it, some had been shot. I felt that it did not matter anymore, that if I had to live through much more of the nightmare then I would be walking into the chambers, for the insanity danced around the edge of my mind all the time, when I viewed my fellow Jews in their terrible conditions, wearing their terrible degrading outfits with the yellow star sewn onto it. JUDE. Since when did a word mean so much scorn and abuse should and could be poured over a person who was born that way? I had no say (I believed) in my birth and upbringing, I believed I was born to Jewish parents because that was the way it was. I know now that I chose that life, those parents, those ordeals but had no way of knowing before I came that I would not be able to cope with it.

You must think of me at that time, dear patient reader, a young man of Jewish background, German in nationality, caught up in a war which was not of my making. Had they asked, I would have gone to war, despite seeing my beloved brother come home a shell, I would have gone to war to fight for my country. Instead they took me from my home, put me on a train, walked me into a camp of walking living skeletons and then proceeded to kill others in front of me. Because I was a Jew.

All my life I had lived with the Jewishness that aroused ire in some 'pure' Germans, it was a problem at school, a problem as I grew up, but I lived with it as part of life, as normal as kosher cooking and Sabbath observance, of candles and of Passover, Hanukah and the Black Fast. I blamed it on the fact we were different and everyone hates that which is different.

But to go to these lengths! To build huge camps – for they were huge, were they not? – and the elaborate gas chambers, the ghastly experiments done on the children, the plundering of the dead, the lengths they went to in providing 'outfits' for us with the hated yellow stars on them, why?

To satisfy some sadistic craving deep within the German people? It was an excuse for some, that we knew well, those who would otherwise have been termed psychopaths, to exert authority, to have a wonderful time at the expense of hapless helpless men women and – heartbreakingly – the children, believing there would be no come back.

And therein lies the whole secret answer, does it not?

Germany was thought to be supreme. The Chancellor said we would win. We would walk all over Europe and into Great Britain. We would conquer the countries who opposed us. We had the greatest army of all time, great war machines which stormed all over the borders of Belgium, Holland and France, which pushed as far as it could into Eastern Europe, taking on the might of the great armies there and suffering great losses and yet they still believed they would win.

And if they did – why, then no one would know about the death camps. No one would know that the Nazi movement sought to eliminate all whom they did not like, from Gypsy to epileptic, taking in every 'strange' race along the way, with particular hatred being reserved for the Jews.

What had we done? Made a success of being businessmen, bankers, financiers, moneylenders – what we turned our hands to we made a success of. Why do people so hate success when it is not they themselves who are successful?

And so they broke our windows one night, they dragged us from our homes, from our loved ones. Gestapo knocked on doors and summoned those within – to walk the path to death.

And death was welcomed by some!

Oh the stories of those who walked with suitcases full of precious possessions, only to lose them. Those who carried their children, only to have them taken from them. Those who believed the chambers were really showers and urged their children into them, living with the screaming which resulted and the sheer horror when they realised what they had done.

No wonder many walked to the wire and were shot.

Would that I had the nerve to do the same thing.

So in my heart I resolved to escape.

I go back to where I was before I diverted onto what you call a 'soap box' to rant and rave for a few moments. I beg forgiveness from my reader. All that is in my heart, I have to say. This is the only way my karma will be resolved and I will be freed from earthbound conditions. I need to clear my mind and my heart of all that hurts me still. For some people, what I have said will be old news, 'yes, read it all, heard it all, get on with it, Daniel.' For others, younger readers, it may be new. The Holocaust, as it is always called, maybe something they have heard of but not fully understood or appreciated.

For it is a human thing to turn away from all bad items on the television or in films. 'Schindler's List' attracted those who were old enough to know what it was all about. Others, younger people, will not have gone, will not know. I write for them as well as I write for those who do know.

Six million Jews died in the camps.

Six million.

It is a number beyond the imagination, beyond belief, beyond comprehension.

And those who killed them had a wonderful time. They called it work, we called it extermination. They called it recreation, we called it torture.

The truly awful and yet enlightening thing which comes out of this is – brave Great Britain fought the Germans on behalf of themselves, and of the French, the Belgians and the Dutch, to contain the might of the German Army within German boundaries. They did not know of the camps until later. I doubt they could have fought any harder had they known! Waging war on land, at sea and in the skies, yes, I have heard the stories since, know of the bravery of so many, the loss of so many. At the time, all we knew was that our beloved country was being bombed by foreigners and yet, I do believe, deep in our hearts we knew our beloved country had to be stopped from its great ideas of taking over half the known world.

I knew nothing then of your great leader, Winston Churchill, of his inspiring and inspired words to keep the British people fighting the war, at home and in Europe. But I know of someone closer to me than he was/is and it is not long now before she features in my life story.

I have to say I know your great leader, Winston Churchill, now. I know also that, when the war was over and peace was restored, there were those who sought to discredit him. Even now some say, 'he wasn't a nice man, was he?' and try to deride and decry his leadership, saying he made this mistake or that, or allowed this to happen with great loss of life – but have they asked themselves what would have happened if he hadn't? Would not the tide of history have flowed another way, would you not now be a different state if he had not taken those decisions, he and the brave men who shared the Cabinet with him at that time?

I have been waiting for my channel to call me to order, for I have once again mounted my soap box and moved sideways from my story! To her credit she has not done so, she is sitting patiently typing the words I give to her, feeling her hands burning and tingling, which is the way she knows it is Spirit who give her the words, they are not from her own mind. Much of what I have said here she has no knowledge of whatsoever. She was a war baby, born in the war years, growing up in the aftermath of war, hearing about it all second hand from those who were there but never experiencing any of it herself. She knows of the Holocaust, of course, but has never met a survivor. She has met someone who escaped before the Gestapo knocked on the door, a brave proud aristocratic lady (now in the Realms) who had to leave everything, including her family, to evade the grasping hands of the terrible men who broke down doors to take what they wanted. But not a survivor.

159

I have brought her face to face with the horrors of man to man. I have presented her with the cold stark facts of the death camps, of the terrible abuse which went on and still there is more to say. And she wonders why she feels down!

But I am aware of her mental and physical condition, dear reader, think not that I push too hard. She had a whole evening of intense and beautiful healing to lift her spirits and heal her aching mind and body and this has worked. She is strong again and ready to carry on. I can tell you now that she is listening to music as she accepts these words, beautiful music which flows like the gentle rivers or the afternoon breezes through swaying branches. I love the music she plays. It distracts her to some degree from the horrors of which she writes. Mind on the music, fingers on the keyboard, words appearing of which she has no knowledge until they appear before her and she corrects the typing mistakes or my slips of grammar. Other than that, she has not altered a single word I have given to her.

There will be many who will doubt this, who will say 'but she writes, so surely she invented all this!' and they should ask themselves whether a gentle lady of her age would invent such horrors.

It comes from Spirit.

It comes from Daniel.

This was Daniel's life.

And Daniel's death – eventually. But before we reach that point, there is much to say still.

Climb down from the soap box, Daniel! It is I who is saying this, not my channel. I know I have diverted but I felt I wanted to say these things.

Right.

I resolved to escape.

A few prisoners had made a mass escape, had aimed for the wire, broken through and were mown down by the guns. The wire was hastily repaired. I knew where it was weak. I knew I wanted to try. They thought – for we overheard them – that the killing of those who ran had deterred us. And for a while we let them think that. We? It was talked of in the hut at night, in whispers. I and two others resolved to try and make our escape. Two young men, of my age and my physical condition. We thought we had a chance.

We picked a moonless night, with some cloud. We did not know we had picked a night when the RAF were mounting huge sorties over Germany but it helped, for the skies were lit with anti-aircraft fire and tracer bullets, with flares and rockets and with the burning of tumbling spiralling aircraft. Many guards were distracted by this. They stood and watched; they were not watching the prisoners.

We ran as silently as we could to the wire, pulled it apart and were through, tugging it back together again as best we could in our haste and our frantic worry that the guns would turn on us.

And we ran like rabbits in the forest, dodging behind bushes and trees, ever fearing the bullet in the back that would end the escape and our lives. Nothing happened. We ran until all three of us had no breath, no strength, no ability to stand any longer. Then we fell face down in the leaves and mud of the great forest and I know I cried into the mud ' I'm free at last!' and wondered if anyone heard.

After we rested for a while, we got ourselves up and plodded on, hoping to find shelter, food, someone to give us some clothes and help us on our way.

It seemed we walked all night. Overhead the planes still roared and we heard the distant sound of bombs exploding, for sound carries in the darkness like no other time. We asked ourselves which town or city was being bombed this night. We asked ourselves if we had a home to go to, should we be fortunate enough to find our way back to our home towns and we all resolved not to try to do such a thing, but to get out of Germany into a neutral country where we could start again.

So we consoled ourselves as we walked, first find help, then look for a way out, a safe way out. We knew of the workings of the Resistance movement in France, we knew there had to be some way of getting out of Germany but how and where was beyond us.

But first things first. Shelter, food, clothes.

We walked in silence, lost in our own thoughts. We walked with lighter tread, for our footsteps led us away from the hated camp.

We saw lights. We ran toward the lights. Dogs barked and people came out, saw us and exclaimed at our thinness, our starved look, our state of health. We looked at one another, we shook hands, we thought we had found a haven.

"Come with us!" urged one man who looked like a farmer, red of face, grey whiskers, sturdy body. And we went with him to a barn where he said we could shelter while he went to fetch food and water.

He returned with Gestapo officers.

I was beaten with rifle butts. I lay on the cold prickly straw, clubbed and kicked and almost unconscious when one lifted his rifle and brought it down on my right hand. It broke every bone in the hand. Then I did pass out.

We were left until morning, locked in the barn. My friends were bleeding and concussed, one had a broken arm, the other had a broken nose and we were all covered in bruises and blood. My hand was useless. The pain was unbelievable. I never knew nerve endings could shriek in such a way. The hand swelled up to three times its size and became a fiery torment which I could do nothing about.

We were all too shocked to speak of the gut wrenching betrayal. For how many pieces of silver had the man sold us down the line? I have yet to meet the man in the realms. I need to meet him, I need to speak with him to clear my mind of the hatred which festered there for so many years. It is gone now but still I would like to speak with him, to examine why he saw fit to hand us over.

Come the first light we were marched back to the camp.

It was a long march. We stumbled along behind an Army truck carrying the Gestapo officers, who laughed and jeered at us as we walked, consumed with pain, dying of starvation and thirst. They drank from billy-cans in front of us, they ate fresh fruit and threw the core and skin at us. They gnawed on meat and gave us not even the bones to chew. One of my friends, a young man called Samuel, the one with the broken arm, could not stand it anymore. He began to run clumsily into the bushes, knowing he would be shot – and he was.

I shouted my anger at them and was ignored. "Jew boys, filthy kikes, fit for nothing," they said aloud so we could hear as we stumbled along, sorrowing for our fallen friend and perhaps wishing we had the nerve to do the same thing.

It was midday by the sun when we arrived. The Camp Commandant was summoned to ask how we had escaped, he was raged at by the Gestapo officers who stalked around the perimeter wire, pointing out weak points here and there, asking how many others had escaped.

"Only the three, sir," he bowed and scraped. We knew if there had been others, he would not have admitted to them and the Gestapo knew this only too well. So they accepted his word and thrust us into a small tin hut which was freezing and left us there.

My friend had a badly swollen face, I had a badly swollen hand. No medical help was given and we expected none. We expected to be killed in front of everyone. We were not. We were released that evening and told to go to our huts.

Later we found out why. Others had escaped and been brought back almost immediately, shot in front of everyone but it had done nothing, others had tried and some had managed to get away during the night. No one had seen them. Those killed in front of everyone were considered martyrs and the commandant feared an uprising.

An uprising, from starved weak people who were kept cowed with guns and wire! An uprising from those whose spirits had been so crushed we had no thoughts left in our heads!

Whatever the real reason, and who would know that? we were allowed to live.

But we paid a price for living. Guards took us for 'play' – we were beaten with rubber hoses, had water forced into our stomachs until we were fit to explode, had electrodes fastened to our private parts and were shocked into insensibility by the force of the charge sent through us. Our toes were stamped on. Our teeth were knocked out of our heads.

Only then were we 'free' to go back to the way we were living before, waiting on the handouts, waiting on the water, waiting on the walk to the gas chambers.

Would that we had gathered the nerve to die out there in the forest!

But if I had, I would not have met the remarkable lady who was to change my outlook on life.

But to do that, I had to go to another camp.

But that is getting ahead of myself.

In the meantime I lived with toothless mouth, bleeding gums, raw tongue, endless agonising pain in my hand which remained unbound and very broken. I lived with black bleak despair and a total lack of understanding of any motive or reason for the way we were treated. Sometimes I ventured to ask a trusty or a

164

guard why they were treating us that way and was met with totally blank looks, for they had not given it a thought. They were not thinking, they were doing and they were doing what they were told, not what they thought was right.

I lived with others who were abused and used, whose bodies were torn apart by multiple penetrations, front and back and mouth, those who were whipped until the blood ran because it pleased someone to string them up and whip them until the blood ran. Others were used as punch bags. Yet others were used for target practice with knives, bayonets or live bullets. We were nothing. We were items to be used and thrown away when we inconsiderately died under their hands, spoiling their games. For that is what they said, "let's play a game!" and some poor soul would be dragged from whatever he or she was doing at that moment and taken away and we would hear the screams for mercy, for an end to the suffering and then the silence when that end came.

And there would be one more empty bunk that night.

We were told we were 'prisoners of war.' The war went on around us, over us, the flights of bombers shrieking through the skies, great black clouds of death and destruction as the Luftwaffe made their way across the lands to Britain, to bomb London and the other big cities and in return we saw and heard the British RAF coming in with their bombs, heard the crunch as another wave hit somewhere. For all we knew, our homes had been flattened, everything we had known and loved and been used to had been reduced to a pile of rubble somewhere, for we were not allowed any news of any kind. We did not know what had been hit and what hadn't. Was Berlin still intact? Was Bonn standing? What of Cologne and Dresden and Duisberg and Potsdam? Every new arrival was asked for news but they all shook their heads and said they knew nothing, they had been held in cattle trucks as we had and knew nothing, heard nothing but what we had heard, the sound of bombs and the waves of bombers, both in and out.

So we were 'prisoners of war' but whose war? If the British had invaded Germany and rounded up all Germans and put them in camps, we would be truly 'prisoners of war' but we were imprisoned by our own people for being our own people. Imprisoned by Germans because we were Germans. We just happened to have another bit tacked on to that, we were German Jews. But did that make us enemies?

I did so want to understand. I gained a reputation for asking questions, guards and officers would point at me and whisper about 'the one who wanted to know.' One officer even invited me into his office to talk, I stood in front of his desk while he reclined, feet on that desk, smoking a fat cigar 'as the British leader, Winston Churchill, does' he told me, blowing aromatic smoke at me and making me long for a cigarette. Odd, I never had smoked but the smell of that smoke at that time made me wish I did, or that I had, for there was no tobacco to be found. On the other hand, if I had been a smoker, that would have been another agony to add to the many already being endured.

I divert myself yet again. I stood in my convict outfit before the gleaming wooden desk, polished that morning by the orderly, one of the men from my hut who had the envied task and gained an extra piece of bread and meat each day for his work. I stood with my right arm and hand in screaming agony, useless, hanging by my side, listening to this officer pontificating about the war, about how Germany would win and wipe French Resistance off the map completely, how we would all storm our way down Whitehall in jackboots, flying the Nazi flag which would be fixed to the gates of Buckingham Palace. He did not answer my question about why we were considered 'prisoners of war.' I did not dare ask him why he had chosen to guard Jews; that would have been taking things a little too far.

So I stood and I listened and I learned precisely nothing.

But did I really expect otherwise?

This man was a sadist, worse than the others. He loved beating women in particular, delighted in calling them out and knocking them to the ground, making them crawl to his boots and lick them clean. Some would be summoned to his office for 'talks', coming back bruised and battered, sometimes with black eyes, sometimes with missing teeth or badly swollen faces. Their breasts would be red and sometimes bleeding from his attentions for he did love to bite the soft female flesh.

He had a hard, ugly face and an arrogant manner that seemed worse than the others and they were bad enough. If I had not been in so much pain and so unhappy standing listening to the drivel which spouted from his mouth, I would have been scheming up a way to remove this person from the face of the earth, even if it meant my own demise. At that point I hurt so much I did not want to live anyway, so what was stopping me walking toward the wire? I don't know. Lack of courage? It took more courage to live than to die, for living meant the daily nightmare of the camp, the deaths, the suffering, the abuse, the torture and torment of the helpless women and children. Fear of what lay beyond death? There we are getting nearer to the truth, I do believe. My faith had gone long before, when so many tragedies stamped their misery on my life; my sister, mother, relatives, brother, then father and Solomon at the cattle pens in Potsdam, then the misery of the camp and those I lost along the way, passing acquaintances, those I was afraid to draw too close to because it was a certainty they would die and I would be bereft again but still they touched my mind and at times my heart. What did the philosopher say? 'No man is an Islande, intire of itself. Ask not for whom the bell tolls, it tolls for thee.'

At that time, to be a Jew in Germany was to be very aware no man was an island, for we were one race persecuted and tormented and tortured and bound for extinction by a race who thought themselves superior to us because they held the upper hand at that time. And because of that, we were as one. So everyone who died took a part of me in any event, whether I wished it or not.

One day we were all hustled and bustled into lines and told to march on out of the gates. No chance to break for freedom, we were too ill, too starved, too weak to do anything but obey. It was Spring, there were small flowers growing along the edges of the path we tramped and I noticed people walked on them. I wanted to shout, 'keep off the flowers!' but it seemed pointless. The plant would still be there when we passed and would grow more flowers if they were crushed. Would we grow more people after we had been crushed, I asked myself. Such foolish thoughts. We were loaded into lorries, the tarpaulins were secured tightly so we could not see where we were going – and could not be seen, either, and we set off in convoy.

Rough roads, potholed and badly maintained, hearing the sound of bombs falling even during the daytime, the clank of something that could have been a tank but we were surely far from a battlefield, we sat in the darkness, lit only by the occasional chinks of light as the tarpaulin moved and fluttered as we hit or bounced over something, we sat in silence, crushed together, many pushed together in a truck designed for far less. But we were all thin, emaciated; we took up little space physically although mentally some of us were giants. Roar of engines, rumble of tyres, shouts and commands, the occasional shot – we were left totally in the dark in so many ways, not knowing where we were going or what was to happen to us.

In the darkness I prayed that the camp would be better than the last, whilst knowing that was highly unlikely. Still, I had to ask, didn't I? Wouldn't you have done the same thing? I guessed we were being taken to another camp, maybe because the war was getting a little close to us, maybe because we were just pawns on the huge chessboard that was Germany in a war situation.

Or maybe because the guards and trusties needed new bodies to play with.

For this is how I came to view the whole situation.

How many views of the war are there?

The generals and colonels, in their offices, the war was a chart on a wall, pins for units moving around here and there, projected advances, losses and gains.

For the people in the stores it meant non-stop work with paper chits, issuing this and supplying that.

For those who kept the vehicles, tanks, planes, lorries and cars, going it meant a lot of maintenance work and scrounging fuel to keep everything on the move.

For the soldier it was shall I live or shall I die?

For those in cities, trying to carry on, it was shall I live or shall I die under foreign bombs?

For the prisoners of war it was scheming to escape Colditz and other prisons.

For the Jews it was a dying nightmare.

For me it was as if we, all of us Jews, had been gathered up and distributed to camps staffed by officers, British and German, and a variety of guards, trusties and others, to play with. Why else would we be treated so?

And on what do I base this feeling?

On the next camp we were taken to.

To be stripped naked, stood in line and forced to watch sexual abuse take place in front of our eyes, to be approached by pouting women, often smoking

169

cigarettes, something we had not seen for years (it felt like years) who came and touched us and stroked us and demanded they use our bodies – women no better than prostitutes making us shamefully aroused and using us for their own pleasures.

As before, it mattered not if the Jewish women were having their monthly problems, their blood was all the better to lubricate the thrusting raping penises of the savages who took them there and then, on the ground, in their offices, in their bunks.

And if they got pregnant, which so many did, they were herded together, bellies swelling and growing with the bastard German child they carried and then we heard the babies were often cut from the living womb and if the women lived – so many died – they were carted off to the gas chambers anyway.

Experiments, that's what they said we were in some cases. I heard first hand of red-hot needles being put in the eyes of children. Why? What possible reason could anyone have to do something so unbelievably nightmarish to an innocent child?

And I did not cry out against this injustice to a child, I did not try to stop the women being abused, I did not try to stop the women handling my body – not that I was ever used, they said I was not big enough for them – for I had become totally numb, inside my head and my heart. I had my faith still, I clung to my prayers and my God as the only lifeline in a world gone mad, a world of savagery beyond anything I could ever imagine.

Back at school, in the days when life was 'normal', we were told of the dark people in Africa, of how they killed and ate human flesh, how they were called 'savages' for they had no civilisation to speak of.

And these people held us in camps and played with us, played life and death games with us, sending us over the edge into insanity and screaming dementia.

And laughed.

170

My faith was all I had. All else was numb. Nothing could, it seemed, disturb me. I was calm, almost rock like inside, I could view the most awful beatings and killings and walk by, or stand as an inanimate mannequin would, watching the life go out of someone I had eaten with that morning and not be moved. I spoke little for there was nothing to speak of to anyone. And I gave silent thanks that Mother, Rosa, Solomon and David had been spared this horror, this world gone mad. I would not have wished such an existence on anyone –

I lie.

I wished it on Father.

But I believed him dead.

I was wrong.

Chapter 14

The new camp was a copy of the old one. Same watchtowers, wretched huts, wire fences, guns and guards. The faces were different; the uniforms were the same. The deaths were the same. Here we – those who were meant to die – were marched away to be put on trains and taken to the gas chambers. But the end result was the same. Death to the Jew.

Our only consolation, if it could be considered so, was that the spring weather meant it was not so bitingly excruciatingly cold. But the spring weather spoke of life, and there was no life in the camp. We were the walking dead.

We had been there – I keep saying we – I mean the group who were transferred from the old camp to this one, despite the fact we were put into huts with those already there, we kept our 'identity' as those from the old camp. I don't know why unless it was the faint sense of familiarity, something to hold on to. We had been there for a few days, maybe a week, when we were all summoned from our hut one morning for an early roll call. As always we carried out the dead to be laid in rows.

And someone in an army uniform walked along the line, poking people with a swagger stick, hitting this one in the stomach, another over the head, because he could.

And when he reached me he stopped dead, his face white, his eyes wide with shock and horror.

It was my father.

I wanted to shout, to scream my agony at him for all that he had done, for all the pain he had inflicted, for the cruelties I suffered. I wanted to shout at him all the abuse I felt inside, for I was burning with hatred for this man who had so callously hurt those I loosely thought of as friends.

But I could not shout. A lifetime in the camp had not only dried my tears, it dried my words too.

The roll call ended, for he walked on, no longer bothering to look at anyone or count the bodies lying on the ground. He just grunted "bury them" and walked off.

I wondered if I would see him again, wondered what the Army was doing with a Jew in an officer's uniform, wondered what I would say, if I could bring myself to speak, wondered what he would say to me.

He found me later, detailed to dig another latrine pit, the shovel taking all my strength for I was so weak, so thin, at that time. He called me over by my number and I looked at him. I do not know what the look said but he flinched. Visibly flinched.

I walked over to him as I had to, for he was an officer and I a mere convict in his camp. He put out a hand which I ignored.

"My son," he said and I ignored that, too. I considered myself no son of his.

"You don't understand..." and I knew that is how it would start. And it did, justification for being a German spy, for informing on our Jewish neighbours, how they had to come for us to cover up his spying activities. When the shop went, he turned to the Germans, after all, he said, he had been making their uniforms for years. And that too had bothered me: why should a good Jewish tailor want to make uniforms for the hated German army when we knew their attitude to our race? But he made the uniforms, and was well paid for them, too, passing on his secret information inside the bundles of jackets and trousers that were collected by Army truck. And after the shop closed, the information went on and he was well paid for it.

And none of us knew a thing about it.

None of us suspected.

I wondered what the golden boy, David, would have made of his father spying for the Germans after his terrible experiences in the war.

I wondered what Solomon would have made of it, he of the deep philosophical mind. Would he have found a way to explain the turncoat our father turned out to be?

But then, none of them knew of the deep sadistic streak in our father, for he never touched them. He only beat me. Daniel, the odd one out, Daniel the clown, Daniel the golden haired dark eyed boy, Daniel the love of his mother's life.

Did that hold the secret, I wonder? Was he jealous?

I stood and wilted in the spring sunshine, wanting nothing more than to lie down and die. I did not want to listen to the justification of a man I had thought of – and still do! – as Poor Father. And indeed he was Poor Father, not able to be himself, having to be a double dealing spy to give himself a status of some kind. The shop never was enough for him and when it folded, then he had nothing, so he sought something and found it in spying.

But to condemn his sons to the camps! That was unforgivable and still is.

I have said I cannot return to the earth plane to work out the karma which holds me there. This is part of it, the hatred I bear for the man who fathered me on the earth plane. I must release it, let it go off into the wildness of hell, wherever that is, the deep dark place where all bad things go. But to do that, I must write it out of my system and my heart and my mind.

He was well fed, well dressed, his hair was cut military style, his hands white and clean. He had strong boots on his feet.

I had nothing.

No food, no clothes, no possessions and very little hair. I had no hope. He had all the hope in the world that Germany would win the war, would walk triumphant over the whole of Europe and he would be a proud part of it.

I did not say I had heard the bombing and knew it wasn't all going as Germany wanted. I did not say I had seen the air fights between the planes and seen the Luftwaffe come tumbling down from the sky. I did not say that one day the world would find out what was going on behind the closed gates of the terrible death camps, although I knew, as clearly as if someone had spoken it to me, that it would happen, that the civilised world would find out and Germany would be forever held as murderers in the sight of all. If I had said any of this, the proud man who stood and lectured me on the future would not have believed a word of it.

He did not look like a Jew any more. He looked like a German. He was passing himself off as a German.

I held his secret, his identity, in my hands.

I feared for my life, for if he was ruthless enough to condemn his sons to the camps – he did not know Solomon would try and make a break for it – he was ruthless enough to have me killed to protect himself.

He held back from that.

In the next shipment out, I was moved out of the camp and out of his life. I never saw my father again.

It was at this point of the book my channel did something she has not done so far – asked me what I thought and felt at this time, asked me to discuss the feelings I had about my father. A difficult thing to do but she knows, from having written this much with me and for me so far, that to fully release my feelings and release myself from the earthbound ties of hatred and unforgiveness, I do need to explore my feelings and expose them to the harsh light of day and to lose them by doing so.

It is difficult, as difficult as it has been to write of the tortures and atrocities which went on in the camps at that time.

But for the sake of my karma, it must be addressed.

What did I feel? At first, nothing but blind hatred and a burning desire to smash in the face of the man who stood before me. How could any man condemn his flesh and blood to the horrors of the death camps? 'Ah but did he know?' my readers will be asking. My answer is this: even if he didn't know and I concede it is likely that he didn't, would human nature not have made him help us escape rather than turn us in? If he wished to be 'taken' and fake a death so that he was removed from the equation as far as our neighbours were concerned, he could have arranged for us to escape into the countryside.

I must divert here yet again, forgive me, dear reader. My channel is puzzled, but I think she knows where this part is to go. And believe it, it is relevant to what I want to say about Poor Father.

My channel was holding a workshop one evening, the type where everyone sitting round in the circle concentrates on just one person to see what they can 'get' as they so carefully phrase it. My channel went round the circle, being given encouraging messages, until she reached the last two. The first, a lady, had a simple message: 'Write the book, Dorothy!' and the second, a man, said he saw a young man or boy hiding from troops among buildings. At that time neither of them knew of Daniel and his desire to write the book. My channel did, but she also knew that at that time I was holding back - even as she was, for the book was tearing us both apart as we worked through my early years – but she knew nothing of my hiding from the troops.

Now I can explain it all. What I have written about the abuse suffered at the hands of my father has resolved the big question mark over why the early years were so traumatic. Yes, we had tragedies beyond those of the normal family, for the most part, but so do other families – they suffer too. There has been an overtone of sadness clinging to those early years that was not explained until I confessed about the way my father treated me.

It was because of the way he treated me I actually ran away from home one time. I hid in the shattered buildings around Potsdam, those left over from the earlier war, the one which claimed the soul and spirit of my beloved brother. I hid and I survived for a whole week, until the local militia were called out to find me.

When they took me home, Father beat me until I was unconscious. Mother thought I had got that way through being assaulted by beggars and ruffians who had found me among the ruins. Mother knew nothing of the way Father treated me. Not once did he warn me not to tell her but somehow I knew that it would be the last thing I did if I ever opened my mouth.

The burning hatred took a while to simmer down but then fear came upon me, the fear he has always induced in me, a fear greater than I had ever felt for here he literally held my life in his hands. No one would say a word if he was to beat me to the ground and then ensure I died in front of him for it was happening daily. And, although dying was something we all learned to live with, I did not want to die at his hands. I did not want him to win. I had silently fought back over many years, a war had gone on between us, a silent unspoken undeclared war but real for all that. I did not want it to end here on the muddy blood-soaked ground of a death camp. It seemed, neither did he, for the speed in which I was arraigned to be deported, as it were, was startling.

It also indicated the degree of power he held.

That poor, round shouldered, put-upon tailor had changed completely. The strutting arrogant sadistic German who paraded around, clouting heads with his swagger stick, shouting orders at all and sundry and expecting instant obedience, was a thousand miles removed from the tailor I had grown up with. But the beatings had revealed the man beneath the dark suit, the savage streak beneath the mild exterior. I knew him as a man with a secret inside but never expected to see it displayed so brazenly before the world. Doubtless it had never occurred to him that anyone he knew would walk into the camp where he held sway.

I wanted to ask what bitterness, what slight, what sense of inadequacy had made him turn against his own people but did not wish to speak.

I wanted to ask how he could treat his sons in such a fashion but that was something I didn't really want to hear. I might not have liked the answer.

I wanted to ask if he had really loved our mother, our Rosa, David and Solomon, how he had really felt when they all died, one after the other but again, I might not have liked the answer.

So I didn't speak to the man I had called Father for so many years.

I could have said 'I forgive you, for you knew not what you did.'

I could have said 'I hold nothing against you, for you are what you are, a weak man looking for a position in life.'

I could have said 'I will never forgive you for what you have done.' But that would not have helped my situation at all.

But now, here in the Realms, I know I must do the hardest thing of all. I must seek out the man who called himself my father and I must give him my forgiveness. Until I do that, I cannot be free.

178

Before then, this book must be written, the story put before the world. Then and only then can Daniel lay aside his convict outfit and don the court jester's outfit instead. Then, wearing his clown's face and mind, Daniel will send out the thoughts that he wishes to see his father. Then there will be a reunion, then there will be understanding, tears and regrets can be washed away in a sea of love and mutual understanding and consideration and Daniel will then be entirely free. There is a way to go yet before that happens. But time has no meaning in the Realms: after all, I searched for over fifty earth years for a circle to accept me until I found my channel and her dear friends!

Going back to where we were, I can say in all honesty that the truck journey out of that camp, leaving behind the people I had arrived with, leaving behind the horror ridden situation of my own father being a guard there, plunged me into the deepest despair I have ever felt, then or since. My one wish was to find a way to get myself shot, a clean death, a clean departure from a world gone so mad there was no sanity left.

We were like pawns. The war was a huge chessboard, with the King and Queen being the Chancellor and his cohorts, the British monarchy were on the other side. In between were the knights, the bishops, the castles – the knights were the politicians doing the advising, together with the Generals who ran the war from safe bunkers, the bishops were the clergymen of all denominations who said God was on their side and that victory was within reach, the castles were the stretches of ground fought over time and again, won by this side and then that and the pawns were the poor soldiers who were caught in the middle, ordered here and there –

My channel watched the Festival of Remembrance in November 2000 as I said she would. (And she cried, as I said she would). During the Festival a 'soldier' recited the Rudyard Kipling poem about Tommy and the thin blue line. I had not been aware of this poem before, but my channel had, for she was nodding in recognition as the man vehemently and passionately spoke the lines. For 'Tommy' read 'Jacques' 'Hans' and any other 'foreign' name you could find. The poem moved me considerably, as it did my channel. Through her, I am learning of wonderful war poetry I never knew existed; I begin to open my mind to the possibility, nay, the certainty! that other people suffered as much as the Germans during the last terrible war, that many who died were young British, French, Belgian and other nationalities. They left behind a legacy of suffering equal to our own. The parade of the war widows moved me more than anything, for they were the ones who had lived with the loss these last 60 or so years.

Somewhere back in the earlier pages of this 'wretched book' as I once described it to my channel, I said my channel had written that the Jews did not have a monopoly on suffering. I accept that fully and whole-heartedly, for the losses sustained by the remainder of the civilised world who joined in the conflict, willingly and unwillingly, were tremendous, were appalling, were unforgivable, were unimaginable. The broken bodies which were laid to rest in the vast cemeteries are like the poppies of the field, only their stones are white. The broken bodies which returned home carry still the scars and wounds of the conflict, after all these years. For many of them now, death is a sweet release from suffering.

I divert! My channel has just gone back through the book, a way to find out where we were, I think in a hint to me to take the book onward, not sideways! So much for not giving philosophy, she is doubtless thinking; here it is in all its glory plastered across these pages! And she is right, of course. Every spirit has something to offer in the way of words of wisdom, these are mine. My thoughts, put together over many years, combined with the new experiences I have had from living so close to my dear sister, are here for you to share, to think about, perhaps to disagree with?   It matters not. What does matter is that they are there, they are put down for all to read.

It is strange. Once in the realms we lose nationality, we are what we are, a discarnate spirit, and yet we still retain the characteristics which formed us during our last incarnation. So I see myself still as a German Jew, and think that way and rationalise that way. It has taken my association with a very English lady to show me that there was another side to the conflict. Never in all the years I searched for a circle to accept me would it have occurred to me to sit with a friend and watch the Festival of Remembrance. Nor would it have occurred to me that there are and were war poets who expressed the suffering in bitter-sweet words. I know there are yet more poems she has not read, but the ones she has are the ones which move her – and me.   The incredible poem "For The Fallen" really says it all. I never knew of such meaningful and wonderful words as those until she introduced them to me and me to them. For that she has my everlasting gratitude, quite apart from the work on the book, which takes its toll of her in migraines and tiredness and at times a disturbed mind, for that of which I write is not pleasant for anyone.

And as she offers all this to me in love, her health, her peace of mind, her time to work with me in this way, so I in turn offer my love to everyone who comes into contact with her, who helps her life along a little, who reaches out to her.   And I say, in all honesty and humility, I am sorry for the war. I am sorry that my people tried to walk across your lands and take your homes for our people. I am sorry for the war dead, for the suffering, for the loneliness and bitterness it has left behind. Wounds such as these are hard to heal, even after all these years. The wounds will be there long after the last survivor of the war has gone to the realms, for your race will never forget the sacrifices made. Never. And nor should you.

I want to give away a small secret of my sister's now. During the two minutes' silence – and what a truly wonderful idea that is! – my sister bowed her head, closed her eyes and before her closed eyes was formed a poppy. It was a gift from me to her. She has told no one of this – now I am telling you. She asked, 'do you really want to say this?' and I said 'yes.' She did not know until this moment that it was my gift to her, either. She knew it was from Spirit, of course, but not who had given it to her. In that moment when your heart grieved for the fallen, dear Sister, I gave you a gift of upliftment. And you took it and you smiled. It was enough.

I have diverted so far! Pawns, I said. Soldiers were pawns in the great war effort, we Jews, we displaced, unwanted, persecuted people were also pawns, moved about at the whim of those who guarded us, who beat us, who tortured us, abused us and killed us.

And so it was I came to the last camp I was to be in. And there the last part of the story begins.

Chapter 15

We have come a long way, my channel and I. She has come through several traumas; I have come to terms with mine. We are working together as one now. Slowly her mediumistic abilities are coming through, as the book is nearing its end and her mind can relax a little from the traumas I have put it through. Her reward will be the closeness with Spirit she wanted and, we believe, still does. To us it is a small thing; to her it is a big thing, so her wish will be granted in the fullness of time, when the book is done, for one! There will be other rewards which she has yet to fully appreciate: recognition of a major piece of work, for one.

During the writing of this book she has come to understand many aspects of Daniel, the reasons why he did the things he did, talked the way he talked, chose the group and the people he did. She understands what he was seeking and when he found it, how happy he was. And is! For the companionship and love I have found will last us both for the rest of our lives – which is in fact eternity. True lasting friendship is very rare – we have found it, it will not leave us, now or ever.

Back then to what she knows I call 'this wretched book' and yet it has released much in me, I am freer and happier than I have been for many, many years, so maybe I should not denigrate it in that way. For all that, there are still dramas and torments to write of which will hurt – as it has all hurt. Which is why I divert so much, to talk to my reader and to give myself a breathing space, as it were, before continuing.

It is also not good for my reader to have unmitigating horror thrown at them, page after page after page. They will despair; they will throw the book down and demand that there be some light relief – which I am providing.

So we came to this new camp. And as we entered its barbed wire gates, ferocious looking dogs, fearsome guards, looming watchtowers, I made a strange decision.

For many of my early years, as I have said, I was Daniel the clown. Then, when Rosa's tragedy happened, when David returned, when things went so horribly wrong, the clown was locked away in a secret place somewhere deep inside my body. I believed I would never be able to be a clown again, everything said that life was a tragedy and there was no place for clowning.

Then, when we were taken, I truly believed there was not even so much as a smile left in this war torn, darkened, gloomy land of ours. Yet, as I sat in a truck full of living skeletons, feeling bones instead of flesh, seeing shaved heads instead of hair, seeing haunted eyes instead of deeply joyful ones, I decided to revive Daniel the clown. After all, I reasoned, life could not get any worse than it already had, so why not try to enliven it just a little for my fellow convicts? We were no longer Jews, we were convicts, prisoners of war, pawns in the war game played by mad men with terrible staring eyes, lightning flashes on their clothes and in their hands, men born of women who knew not what they had brought into this world gone totally completely mad.

So, when the truck ground to a shuddering halt and the order was given for us to get out, I fell out. I heard laughter. God, in a place of horror I heard laughter. And it did something to me, it lifted me. I lay on the ground, grinning like a demented creature, watching the smiles. Then, with a bound I was up again. As we were marched off to our hut, I pretended to fall over my feet which brought more laughter from the guards.

"We have a clown in our midst!" said one, pointing to me. The others laughed, even ones who had not seen my pretend stumble. Laughter rippled through the air like a breath of summer. For a moment the bleakness lifted, and then came back down again.

It didn't matter. I knew I could do it.

I knew I would do it again, too.

Lying awake on narrow planks, listening to the breathing, sobbing, moaning, keening sounds which had filled every night since I was first taken, I planned my strategy.

Believe me, I had no intention of doing this for extra rations, for favours, for the hope of life, for in those camps none of this was of value. Should I be given extra rations, I would have to share it or be an outcast. Favours, ditto. Hope of life, that was extinct. Everyone knew that. This was ethnic cleansing on a huge scale. Modern term, old disease.

I wanted to do it for me, first and foremost. I did not want to go to my death feeling as if every day had been wasted, that I had given nothing to those around me. Selfish thoughts, I wanted to go to my Maker with at the very least a recommendation that I did something at the end to justify my existence.

I wanted to uplift myself. I was suddenly sick and tired of being so far down that there was nowhere else to go but up.

Second, I wanted to do it for the strangers I found myself with, for every one of them was a fellow convict. Sharing with me the horrors of the camp, the pain, the suffering, the mental torment, the sheer anguish of the inevitability of death coming sooner or later.

Third, and perhaps this is the most important of all, I wanted to show them, the Nazis, the Gestapo, the SS, anyone else who came anywhere near me, that they had not crushed my spirit or my soul. It was still there, it was still intact; it was still a spark of life they had not managed to stamp out of existence.

And so I dreamed and planned and schemed.

First rule: never to speak to them.

Second rule: make like they weren't there.

Third rule: make it as stupid as possible so that others would laugh, if only for the merest fraction of a second. It would inspire them a little.

Mime was the only answer.

And so I began the last phase of my life as a clown.

It almost seems wrong to describe it as a phase, yet looking back, that is how it seemed to me. For it began with an intention and ended with an intention, too. So yes, it is a phase.

My readers will be asking what I did as a clown, how I manifested myself in that phase. Well, it was simple.

"Come here!" was met with my 'walking' into a sheet of glass, unable to get past it, until I found a 'doorway' and presented myself, bald, emaciated, starving, hurting – for although the hand had healed to some degree, it had healed crooked and often ached abominably – before whoever had summoned me for whatever reason. They would stand, bemused, at my antics, then a smile would appear and then a laugh. Fellow convicts would stand and openly grin at me. It lifted their spirits for a moment which is all I sought to do.

Sent on an urgent errand, I would stumble over my feet, or pretend to have an aching broken back that prevented me standing upright and would take my time.

I would find a stick and pretend to climb it, falling back to the ground all the time.

Did it hurt? Sometimes, if I fell badly, sometimes I fell on the hand which hurt but gritted teeth allowed no sound to escape.

Did it work? I was not asked to do urgent errands any more.

Asked to speak, I would indicate a throat cutting and shake my head. They believed I had lost my voice for no one had heard me speak from the time I was taken through the sour gates of the sour prison which was my final home. I had not spoken on the journey, having no desire any more to befriend anyone, only to see them die, or transported from the camp, or beaten and crushed and abused. Seeing it all the time was bad enough, seeing it done to people you had spoken to, shared bread with, given a space in a queue, made a part of your life by the tiniest courtesies that still seemed to govern life inside the madhouse.

For some weeks this was the way I lived, the way I intended to wait out the war, in the hope I could return to Potsdam when it was all over and try and pick up the pieces of life and start again.

I didn't think my father would dare return to the place he had known and worked, for many would have found out about his treachery. I believed I would be safe there, if only –

If only the bombing would end the war, if only Germany would capitulate, as it had to, for it was clear from snatches of conversations and the many aircraft, foreign aircraft, we saw overhead, that all was not going Germany's way.

If only we could believe that we prisoners of war would be allowed to go free, but did we know too much, would we talk too much of our inhuman treatment in the camps?

If only I thought there was a Potsdam to go back to.

A life to pick up and start again.

Treating this as an intermission, a mere phase, was not easy but it was a way to cope in nightmare madness of pain, suffering, abuse, torture – both mental and physical – of the slaughter of the innocents which went on daily.

So I played the fool and got by – just.

And then I met a wonderful lady. And everything I had thought and planned went out of the nearest open freezing cold window.

There were many women in the camp.

There was no question of my getting involved with any of them, for to see a woman killed is almost worse than seeing a man killed and I saw enough of both to last me a lifetime of nightmares. To see a woman abused is worse to me than seeing a man abused for women should be nurtured and cared for, not raped in both vagina and anus, to appease and slake the guards who took the women as they wished.

This one lady had attracted my attention by her bearing. Unlike the others, she did not walk with cowed bowed head and bent shoulders. She walked proud, even if she walked at a shuffle, as if in considerable pain. She held both hands inside her tunic, again as if she was in pain. Sometimes her face was swollen, sometimes her eyes were closed by bruises. Sometimes she walked as if she too had been raped; the women developed a walk which made it clear what had happened to them.

No matter how she walked, what she was enduring in bruises and marks, she was proud. I grabbed one prisoner's arm, gestured to her and raised my eyebrows in question.

"Odette," he said. "Odette, the British spy." And walked off to continue his task, whatever it was he had allocated to him or had allocated to himself that day.

Odette. I began to follow her, dancing along in her footsteps, hoping she would turn and look at me. She didn't, for ages, too busy being proud and looking ahead at where she was going, defying anyone to stop her.

Then one day she did stop, turn and look at me, busy imitating her walk.

"That isn't funny," she snapped. "Who are you, anyway?"

I danced a little, did a somersault (which hurt my bad hand something really bad but I tried not to let on) and she almost smiled.

"Oh, the clown." I nodded. "Don't you talk?" I shook my head.   "Because you can't, or because you don't want to?"

Double question, almost impossible to answer. I shook my head and then nodded, hoping she would understand.

"I see," she said. "Silence is golden and all that."

I nodded again.

"Well, clown, what do you want of me?"

What a question! What did I want of a lady so proud, so upright, so defiant? Some of her strength? Her friendship? Her understanding? I could not answer for I did not really know. I tipped my head to one side and smiled. And by a miracle she understood.

"You want us to be friends." A flat statement but a true one. I nodded. "What an interesting idea, a friend in a place like this." A sweeping glance around the stinking huts in which we existed, the trampled mud of the ground underfoot, the wire fences, guards, dogs, guns and watchtowers. It was an interesting idea and a daring one, for to make friends meant making a chance at abject misery, suffering and sorrow if it all went wrong and one died.

Then she smiled. When Odette smiled at me, the world lit up. The sun came out, the guards disappeared and pure radiance shone around me. I don't know if anyone else ever saw it but I did. And in my heart there burned something I thought had gone forever – love.

"Come, clown," she ordered and we walked slowly, together.

And so began my relationship with the beautiful, the proud, the stubborn, the arrogant and the courageous Odette.

189

Odette wrote her own book when she was finally back in England after the war. She wrote then of her tortures, the pulling out of her finger – and toe-nails, an agony none of us can begin to even come close to visualising. The abuse, the rapes, the beatings, the deprivation which almost turned her mind. You will find it all in her book, those who wish to know more.

But on the walks we took together, secretly at times, she whispered to me all of that and more. And it is the 'and more' that I have to bring to you, my reader, along with the tragedies of my own life. For this book is to settle Odette's karma as much as my own.

Imagine, if it is at all possible for you, the reader, to do so, being locked in a cell, minus your finger and toe nails, each pulled out agonisingly, one after the other, a pain which could and almost did wreck her mind. And then to be beaten about the head and body, she, this beautiful soul, damaged so much in her body through the terrible injuries they inflicted in trying to get her secrets from her.

And then, the emptiness of the cell. The loneliness of the passing hours, the torment of the pain which would not lie down and let her rest.

And then to have them come, the men, one after the other, to rape, to abuse, to torment and to verbally abuse this high born lady from the aristocratic family, to treat her like a whore, to tell her she was such a being – and to tell her this in two languages, German and English, and here it is said loud and clear by Daniel, for Odette cannot bring herself to say it – the English was spoken by the officers who took their share in the abuse and the rape.

I want to take a step back here to applaud all women for their strength of character and mind. But most of all to applaud the women I admire the most; Odette for her outstanding courage and pride which carried her through this appallingly terrible time, an ordeal only equalled by my own, I do believe: my friend the beautiful lady, who has suffered so much, lost so much, yet goes on giving endless devoted service to Spirit even though she declares she is an unwilling medium - and my dear channel. At the time of writing this, she is playing Celtic New Age music, uplifting, full of dancing rhythms and mysteriously beautiful sounds which enchant me as much as they are enchanting her and she is doing this for she is writing less than one week after a bereavement which has shaken her and all around her. And she has continued to work with Daniel through her grief and sorrow at the passing. Each, in their own way, have shown exceptional courage and strength of character. Would that some men would be as strong as they are!

And so we came into summer. The leaves on the trees outside the camp were green, the air above the camp was thick with death and destruction, for the killing went on relentlessly, day after day after miserable endless day. More Jews arrived, more Poles, more dispossessed and displaced people who had done nothing but offend in sight those of the Nazi regime who wished them gone. And somehow Daniel the clown managed to go on clowning, falling, dancing, miming his way through the days and not speaking became a way of life. Not speaking became a life-giving thing, for soon they did not expect replies but looked for and found nonsense instead. Not one stopped to look into my eyes which Odette told me were haunted and sad and sorrowing all at the same time. But they looked no further than the idiot smile I plastered on and kept fixed on for the entire day sometimes, until a rictus of muscles told me it was time to stop, to resume the serious face that clowns often wore.

And I grew thinner and Odette grew thinner and we starved together and shared together and suffered together, for they would not leave her alone.

Then one day she was not there.

Gone.

No one knew or seemed to know, but then was I asking the right questions with my no voice questions? All I knew was she had gone and the light had gone out of my life. I did not know if she lived or was dead of the abuse they gave her. I knew not and I cried within.

The camp was empty for me. I had not realised how I had come to look for that shambling broken walk of hers, the proud smile, the radiant smile when she saw me, the quiet voice that whispered of horrors and yet made it seem like a scary tale to tell a child rather than something unbelievably savage and real.

And at that time there seemed to be an air of urgency about everyone. More and more people were taken away to the chambers, more and more truckloads were taken out as if the guards were anticipating something, the end of the war? And their job had to be done before it ended, or they would be left with thousands of witnesses to their cruelties. And somehow the urgency came upon them all and there were more rapes, more beatings, more savagery than ever. Even this poor clown, once the butt of jokes only, was beaten almost every day, my hand broken yet again, for it seemed to amuse them to break something which was already obviously broken.

It was at that time I knew I had to make an effort to escape one more time, for I did not dare walk into the gas chambers, does that sound foolish to my readers? I think it was because I was determined not to be a sheep, to allow myself to be walked into death with others as if I had no mind of my own.

With the urgency that was going on, the guards were becoming lax, not watching the gates or the wire as much as they did before. Whether this was because they wanted their share of the action – to use a modern phrase – before the end came or just sheer carelessness, I had no way of knowing for I would not speak to them or with

192

them. So I watched and waited and hesitated sometimes, not sure if the moment was right to make my break for it. Several did and were shot down, so I waited a while longer, all the time hurting so much that it really felt as if it did not matter whether I lived or died. All that was precious to me had long gone, even Odette had gone.

The moment came one overcast almost rainy day when the gate was open just a fraction for a lorry had come through and no one had secured the catch once again. I moved closer to the gates, saw no one was watching and then broke through and ran. And knew, by the shouts, that others were running with me, others had taken the chance I had.

Running through soft grass, running through trees, dodging here and there, hearing the sound of guns – hearing the shouts – feeling a terrible tearing pain that seemed to go through from one side to the other, from back to the front, saw the blood fountaining from me, knew that it was the end after all.

There was blackness, intense blackness for the shortest time and then I found myself standing by a tree, looking down at a shattered body with three holes in its back. I saw the men come, the guards, who turned the body over with boots that were splattered with rain from the soft grass I had so recently run across, saw them crouch down to record the number tattooed on its arm, saw them grin at one another, heard the words 'one less to worry about' and saw them turn and walk away, back to the camp, back to the horrors and the savagery and the lust and the torment that no longer was mine to trouble about.

And I stood and looked down at the body, so thin, so fragile, so helpless in death that it looked like a doll in a tattered nightdress. The water on the grass seeped into the convict uniform and stained it grey, as grey as the skin on the body. I had not realised how thin I had become, nor how grey and ill looking.

And I did not know what had happened to me. I knew I was alive and yet there was my body lying on the ground, unwanted, uncared for, unburied. I looked round, seeking direction, not knowing what to do and saw some people coming toward me, people I vaguely recognised. They waved, they called and I started to walk toward them, consciously avoiding the trees and bushes but realising they were walking right through them.

When they reached me, I saw within the radiance which surrounded them that I was looking at Rosa, Solomon, David and Mother.

And then I cried.

And so the story closes.

For a long moment there my channel was too overcome to continue. She had to close down her box of tricks and go and look at something else: her collection of music on what I have learned to call CDs, the silver discs which contain so much wonderful and magical music to delight the ears.

The story closes and yet doesn't close, for there is much to be said yet on my search for a circle to take me. And that I will do, but not this night, for we have gone far enough and for long enough for my channel and myself to need a break. And to blink back tears which are bothering both of us at this time.

It has been hard going, this telling, criminally hard on both of us. But the relief that it is done, that the final line of the earth part of the story has been put in place, is incredible.

From here on it is all spiritual talk and that is much easier, if equally sad at times, than the first part.

I stood among the trees of the forest, aware of the sound of birds such as I had never heard before. They sounded like rippling water, like all the music of the world combined together. I stood with the tears pouring down my face as if they would never stop coming from me and with them drained the hurt, the suffering, the pain and torment I had been through. I cried and yet my skin was not wet. The tears evaporated into the soft afternoon air, sweet as sunshine in summer.

And then Mother was there, her beautiful calm face in front of me, Rosa was there, same as ever, David, smiling his golden smile and Solomon, serious as ever and they said together "so, you have come home at last!" and there were hugs and kisses and smiles and arms to hold me up. And the hated convict outfit had disappeared and in its place was a robe of pure silk which was luxury to feel against my skin. I felt clean, felt refreshed, rejuvenated. And we walked, or I call it walking but somehow we were travelling so fast across the grass that our feet left no marks behind. I saw the hated wire fence of the camp, but it had no power to touch me anymore. And then we seemed to fly somehow, I am not sure even now how it happened but we were no longer on the earth, we were walking across grass which was so intensely green it almost hurt. And there was a collection of people all waiting, smiling, some waving and in a flicker of a moment I knew it was Grandfather Luka, grandmother at his side and there were my aunts and uncles and my other grandparents and a boy I had known at school and a dog I once helped because it had a cut paw and I cried all over again.

My first real thought was: had I know how wonderful it was here, I would not have fought to stay alive throughout the nightmare time in the camp.

My second thought was: I have to let others know about this somehow.

But before I could really ask anyone about anything I was moved quickly to the Hospital area, where they took care of me, fixed my damaged hand, my aching body, my starved body. In no time the resting period was over and I was back among my relatives and friends, delighting in the colours and perfumes of this new world.

This happy state lasted for some time. Then, for some reason, the whole incarnation began to return. I began to relive every moment of it, the pain, the beatings, the sadness, the losses, the torture and I knew I was a very long way from being mentally healed. I asked myself over and over why I should have had to endure so much, what had it all been for.

No one argued with me about my feelings, for it is for each soul to find its own path. I had a small house where I lived in relative peace, but the walls were blank and became screens for my ever troubled mind to play out the visions of the life I had endured.

Wiser spirits suggested I might wish to return, to take up another incarnation, but this I refused to do – and still do! – for fear of finding myself in a similar or even worse predicament this next time.

Other spirits asked me to rationalise just what it was that gave me the problems I could not settle in my mind.

After much thought I came to the conclusion that it was the sheer senselessness of the whole dreadful nightmare of the Holocaust which had so disturbed me. It was widely known throughout the Realms that six million people died; an unbelievable number by anyone's reckoning. It was also widely referred to as the Holocaust and each spirit who came from that Godforsaken place were treated with great care and tenderness, for they knew how we had suffered.

I was also aware of a deep anger and hatred for my earth father which had to be eradicated before I could truly at peace.

How then to sort myself out?

Grandfather Luka gave me some idea when he said: "the world should know how you suffered, Daniel." From that comment the thought came of a book, to tell the truth, to put it before the people of the world.

But books are written by special people, those who have knowledge enough to put the words in the right place in front of the right people. Books are written by channels who are sensitive enough to be able to accept the impressions and words given by a discarnate spirit and put them in book form.

And before any of that could happen, I needed to find a circle to accept me, to find out whether there was anyone within that circle to write the book.

Would you believe, my reader, it took me fifty earth years to find such a circle?

Oh, I drew close to many a vibration of light reaching to the realms, came in to uplift and to give laughter and was given love and told to move on. For the longest time I despaired of finding a circle, of finding anyone who would accept me, let alone write a book for me.

Fifty years of earth time. It is but the flicker of an eyelid in the sight of the Spirit world, where time has no meaning but for me it seemed an eternity of searching.

Then I was drawn to a circle sitting in that most spiritual of places, that little island off the coast of England. I had drawn close there before, wondering if it was right. When I saw my portrait being drawn, I knew I had to come close.

She may not understand this, but my sister's laugh triggered my feelings that night. She laughed with me, laughed at my jokes, told me to come again and I knew I would, for I needed that warmth, that feeling.

And she welcomed me every time. Welcomed me with honesty and truth and love. No false encouragement there to come and visit, it was real. I tried impressing her with the thought of a book and received encouragement.

The patience, the understanding, the love she has shown throughout the writing of this book has been overwhelming.

Now the book is written. As far as I am concerned, this 'wretched book' is done. It is done this December, 2000. I can have a happy Christmas for the first time in my life. Now the burdens have rolled away, now the hatred, the anger and the hurt are finally gone, written out, ready to be put before the world. This Christmas I can visit my sister, be with her when she opens her gifts, delight with her in the light and happiness of the season which she loves, knowing my hurting days are finally done.

The convict outfit is burned in the fires of pure love.

The court jester is here, my sister, ready to dance to your tune of joy of life.

Your clown will shed no more tears.

End-piece: from Odette

8th December 2000

Every book needs an 'end-piece' if it is not a work of fiction and this is far from being a work of fiction, although to those who are not of the understanding it will seem that way. At the beginning of this book Daniel tells his channel, the patient and loving sister, that he cannot claim to have the book as his own work, that he has worked with another. Indeed he has, he has worked with me and whilst the words may not always have been his, the story is his alone and the hurt, the tears and the suffering which has spilled onto these pages is also his alone.

It has been a work of pure courage to commit such a terrible life story to paper, to present it to a world which may not believe a single word of it, but I am saying that every part of it is true, for I have lived the book with Daniel, lived the telling and the sadness it gave him. I helped him to find the healing he needed and in fact gathered the family around him so that he would find and gain the courage needed to complete the work. For Daniel is one of the special spirits, an old soul with a thousand incarnations behind him who was so severely damaged by this last visit to the earth plane that he was almost in despair, which for a spirit is a very sad thing indeed. The long search he had for acceptance almost completed the despair until he came across the loving vibration which I have now sensed and followed myself, to find the love and acceptance he found.

This deeply emotional book has been written through some deeply emotional times on both sides of the divide, for as we have battled with Daniel's own despair, sadness and heartache in retelling a terrible life, so our sister has had her own problems: the ups and downs of business life, constant migraines and bereavements all making her burden as heavy as ours seemed to be at times.

But – it is a fact that Love conquers all and we have, every one of us, gained something from the experience, not least our sister herself, who has the knowledge now that she is capable of channelling a book as easily as she once channelled the voice of Daniel himself – with a little pushing - and has a book to market that she can be proud of, for it is a work of great importance and significance in the Spiritualist movement as well as interesting to those outside the understanding of the great truths.

The book itself is a living testament to the statement *There Is No Death – Life Is Eternal.*

Blessings be upon all who read this book, may your lives be enriched with the knowledge of the great truth and the love of Spirit be with you always.

Odette